CREATE THE SUSPENSE FILM

THAT SELLS

D0067064

CREATE THE SUSPENSE FILM THAT SELLS

FOR YOU -
- THE PRODUCER -
- DIRECTOR -
- WRITER -

RENÉE HARMON

CIARA PRODUCTIONS

The information contained in this book is of an educational nature.

First Edition 2000
Published in the United States of America
by Ciara Productions Publishing Division

Library of Congress Cataloging-in-Publication Data

Renée Harmon
CREATE THE SUSPENSE FILM THAT SELLS

Includes references and index
ISBN 0-9673253-0-7

Cover Design by Sandy Woo

Jostens Printing and Publishing

Printed in the United States of America
Jostens Printing and Publishing

Visalia, CA 93278

CREATE THE SUSPENSE FILM THAT SELLS

FOR YOU
- THE PRODUCER -
- DIRECTOR -
- WRITER -

RENÉE HARMON

CIARA PRODUCTIONS

Los Angeles

OTHER BOOKS BY THE BESTSELLING AUTHOR RENÉE HARMON

Film Directing: Killer Style and
Cutting Edge Technique

The Beginning Filmmaker's Guide
to a Successful First Project

Teaching the Young Actor

The Beginning Filmmaker's Business
Guide

The Beginning Filmmaker's Guide to
Directing

How to Audition for Movies and TV

Low Budget Films that Sell

The Complete Book of Success

The Actor's Survival in Today's Film

TABLE OF CONTENTS

INTRODUCTION

Why didn't your friend's film win a film festival award...
Why...
Why was the major studio production suddenly pulled from distribution and ended on the shelves of video stores... Why...
Why do a number of mediocre TV series keep their audience appeal for years... Why...

"Well," you shrug, "how should I know?"

Hold your horses and read on.

The success of any SUSPENSE film depends on the symbiotic relationship between viewers and the events happening on the screen. Possibly both, your friend and the experienced producer/director, failed to base their decisions regarding story line, characterization, mood and environment upon their films all powerful SUSPENSE core. SUSPENSE is the organizing force that not only sets up complications, but holds the SUSPENSE film together. The selling SUSPENSE film tops each obstacle put into the hero's way, as pivotal scenes (Plot Points) not only change situations but change dynamics and relationships between characters. In short: keep your viewers entertained and thrilled. Besides providing highly dramatic events, gripping visual action and powerful conflicts between characters, the selling SUSPENSE film explores some aspects of the human mind and soul, as the hero struggles to find the answer to an unresolved question.

Within the framework of this genre we are dealing with the following categories:
* WHO DONE IT - WHY DONE IT- HOW DONE IT
  ** Police Procedural
  ** Private Investigator (PI)
  ** Amateur Sleuth
* ACTION FILM
* HORROR FILM
* SUSPENSE DRAMA

CREATE THE SUSPENSE FILM THAT SELLS focuses upon the specifics each SUSPENSE genre demands, it illuminates the SUSPENSE film's structure and deals with SUSPENSE characterization, dialog, point of view, and most importantly, environment (light, sound and camera moves).

The full length screen play FROZEN SCREAM - feature film (Ciara Productions, Los Angeles, 21st Century Distribution Corporation, New York) serves as a guideline for the topics discussed in each chapter.

And now let's roll up our sleeves and go to work.

*

PART I

SUSPENSE FILMS

WHO DONE IT - WHY DONE IT - HOW DONE IT

Now we are dealing with the seedy aspects of life, gang fights, bank robberies, murder, kidnapping, white color crime, to name a few. Today's WHO DONE IT - WHY DONE IT - HOW DONE IT concentrates on the professional detective, the Soft Cloth man who is part of a team, the licensed Private Investigator and at times on the Amateur Sleuth. The "mastermind loner" of bygone years is out of the picture. The following "ingredients" will keep your WHO DONE IT - WHY DONE IT - HOW DONE IT exciting and thrilling:

* Hook, unique situation
* Main character's motivation leading to goals
* Main question demanding an answer

The filmmaker deals with these suspense categories:

OPEN MYSTERY: The viewer knows who the culprit is and enjoys watching the investigator/ detective solve the crime.

CLOSED MYSTERY: The viewer doesn't know who the culprit is. There are several suspects.

The above categories are broken down into these subcategories:

WHO DONE IT: The viewer is interested in seeing a baffling crime solved. Background, environment and mood are important.

WHY DONE IT: The plot is character based. Characters are fascinating but believable.

HOW DONE IT: Though the plot indicates who the culprit is, he/she cannot be brought to justice. Present the crime in a way the viewer <u>thinks</u> it was committed, but not the way the crime <u>actually</u> happened. Do not reveal this information until you have reached your film's denouement.

Never combine two different stories for your WHO DONE IT - WHY DONE IT - HOW DONE IT but connect Main Plot and/or Sub Plots by answering these questions

* What is the story (plot) all about?
* Is the Sub Plot important to the story?
* Does the Sub Plot provide the emotional layering necessary to the plot? Emotional layering is important for the Amateur Sleuth film. The protagonist must have an emotional reason to get involved.
* Protagonist's (hero's) NEED resulting in goal
* Antagonist's (villain's) NEED resulting in goal
* Who or what is keeping protagonist from reaching goal
* Protagonist's internal conflict (if applicable)
* Antagonist's internal conflict (if applicable)
* Protagonist's personal relationships (if applicable)
* Antagonist's personal relationships (if applicable)

3

* Protagonist's desires and aspirations unrelated to the mystery on hand (if applicable)
* Antagonist's desires and aspirations unrelated to the mystery on hand (if applicable)
* Conflict between protagonist and opposing forces (forces known)
* Conflict between protagonist and opposing forces (forces not known)
* Conflict between protagonists and goals (no one believes him/her)
* Conflict between protagonists and reality (subjective versus objective reality)

Handle the protagonist's (hero) ATTITUDE carefully. If, because of the plot line, your hero's ATTITUDE (emotional, psychological and/or behavioral) changes, do not spring this change upon the viewer suddenly, but plant it in previous scenes. Characterization must grow stronger during Act II. Show character facets the viewer did not expect or strengthen the ones the viewer is familiar with.

Regardless whether the antagonist (villain) is a sociopath, a psychopath or a seemingly ordinary person, always reveal his/her fatal character flaw. A villain may be complacent on the surface, but behind this calm exterior smolders a volcano. The antagonist believes strongly in the validity of his/her goals may these based on self-justification, rationalization, greediness or individual belief.

POLICE PROCEDURAL

Portray streetwise cops. Deal realistically with the precinct routine. And don't forget the detective's personal life, his/her family, friends and foes. Give each of these minor characters a life of their own, but do not have them overshadow the crime your film deals with.

The detectives, the "Soft Cloth" men, emotionally speaking, come in all sizes and shapes. Create believable human beings who hate and love, who have flaws and good points. Police detectives work under enormous stress. Needless to say, the tension they are under causes difficulties in their personal life. Many detectives are divorced or are unable to form a close relationship. Among themselves they have developed a bizarre and seemingly callous "galgenhumor" (gallows humor) that helps them to do their job.

A POLICE PROCEDURAL film demands research. Lots of research. The filmmaker must learn about a detective's duties and area of expertise. It helps to be familiar with the detective division's organizational structure:

* Operations Bureau
* Detectives: Robbery, homicide, burglary, general investigations
* Vice: Prostitution, gambling

Precinct detectives conduct a crime's initial investigation. The detective division continues the investigation beyond the preliminary stage.

ARMS. The official police sidearm is a .38 caliber Smith and Wesson revolver with a four inch barrel. "Soft Cloth" men carry a .39 two barrels for easier concealment.

CRIME SCENE SEARCH UNIT. Lifts fingerprints. Photographs the crime scene. Recovers bullets and fragments. Casts footprints, tire marks and blood evidence.

4

Swabs for gunpowder residue. Sweeps scene with evidence vacuum cleaner. Catalogs evidence. Takes fingernail scrapings of victim. Immediately upon arrival at the crime scene the detective records: Time of police arrival, weather conditions, crime scene's address.

SEARCH WARRANT: Only if the detective has "probable cause" and lists the reasons for this "cause" will a judge issue a search warrant.

HOW TO DEAL WITH THE SNITCH. Never have your detective meet him/her at the police station. Always change meeting places and have the detective pay the snitch with cold hard cash. Checks are out. If any possible have your detective verify the received information: Does the snitch seem reliable and is the given information consistent.

MAKING AN ARREST. Forget about threats. Approaching the suspect, the detective must watch the suspect's hands for a weapon.

IDENTIFICATION. After the initial crime scene investigation, further steps are taken to identify a victim via dental records, medical records, identifying documents, fingerprints and clothing, such as labels and dry cleaning numbers.

INTERVIEW VERSUS INTERROGATION. The person to be interviewed is usually a witness or the victim himself/herself. Since human factors affect any interview, the detective should interview witnesses as soon as possible. At times he/she might deal with a reluctant witness because of fear of self-incrimination, friendship with the suspect or dislike of the interviewing detective.

Others may welcome the attention given to them. These are the publicity seekers, false accusers, liars and self-important fictionalizers.

At times an interview may lead to an interrogation. The interrogation involves a suspect. Interrogating a suspect the detective must remember that every suspect is protected by the 5th Amendment. This applies to the interrogation as well as to the interview. Yes, interrogation scenes present a challenge to the filmmaker. But stay away from the "Good Cop - Bad Cop" routine, viewers are tired of it. Concentrate on the "personality" technique: Adjust the detectives personality to the suspect to be interrogated. The detective takes time, watches the suspect, smiles, offers coffee and makes some small talk while observing the suspect's body language. Create a detective who shows understanding for the crime under investigation. At best your detective appears sincere and impartial.

PRIVATE INVESTIGATOR (PI)

Most PI's have extensive background in police work, the FBI or even CIA. Such a background, though helpful, is not necessary. PI's coming from a wide range of professions and occupations have to survive without the benefit of police experience. Not every one is qualified to open a detective agency. Contact your local police or sheriff's department for specific requirements. There are rules and regulations to be followed. These regulations differ from state to state. New York, for instance does not permit a PI to call himself/herself Private Detective, since this is a police rank. In California a PI cannot investigate a homicide without police permission. Most states require the PI to carry liability insurance. Next he/she needs a Security Bond to protect clients in case of failure to live up to the contractual agreement.

If your PI carries a weapon comply with state regulations. Visit a local gun shop to get the information you need.

Besides a cellular phone, camera, binoculars, flashlight, knife and credit cards (to open doors), a fax machine and e-mail the filmmaker might provide the PI with these "toys": Briefcase with secreted tape recorder, infinite transmitter to pick up conversations, police scanner, micro bugs.

Contrary to what films make us believe, the PI's work is rather humdrum and ordinary. Mostly the PI is hired to: find missing persons (relatives, abused wives, stressed out elderly, people with mental problems), locate missing documents, find runaway teens (most leave because they are unable to cope with the home environment), provide security, collect outstanding debts, and do the attorney's or insurance company's footwork.

While the PI might encounter danger during any of the above assignments, it is the Bounty Hunter, going after escaped prisoners, bail jumpers and felons who is always at risk.

Most PI and Bounty Hunting assignments require SURVEILLANCE:

ON FOOT. Contrary to what we see in films, following a person on foot is nearly impossible. You may use this surveillance method in a limited way as your PI follows a person within a hotel or an office building.

IN A CAR. This means team surveillance. Two cars are necessary. Via phones the drivers stay in contact. One car drives parallel to the suspect's car, the second car drives behind it. Possibly involve a third car. This surveillance method works best on freeways and on the open road.

STATIONARY. The PI needs binoculars and a camera with telephoto lens, camcorder as well as a high tech listening device.

UNDERCOVER: Dangerous for the PI in real live, but exciting to watch on the screen. The PI infiltrates the suspect's camp. This type of surveillance requires considerable groundwork, not only does the PI need a new identity (phony driver's license and social security card) provided by a high priced "fly by night" operator, but the infiltrating PI must be well versed in the prevailing jargon, dress code and behavior of the "camp" to be invaded. In short, the PI must be a skilled actor.

Forget about the "generic" PI, the tough but sensitive guy whom we have seen in films and read about in novels over and over. We are sick of him/her. Make your PI a living, breathing, human being. Give your PI flaws, eccentricities, aspirations and desires that have nothing to do with the case on hand. But be careful, never permit your PI's life and loves, his/her joys or heartbreaks and personal dreams to overshadow the suspense story.

Most likely your PI works on more cases than the one depicted in your film. Some cases, granted, are more challenging than others, but avoid your PI's emotional involvement.

While your PI, supposedly, remains within the borders set by law, another type - the COWBOY - doesn't. This character might either be your PI's secret associate or his nemesis. Either way the Cowboy adds spice to your film. He/she "performs" in a way the PI can't or won't. The Cowboy doesn't care. Kidnapping, illegal searching, seizing of property or evidence, threatening during an interview, bodily harm, you name it, he/she does it.

AMATEUR SLEUTH.

The Amateur Sleuth is a private citizen who, for some reason or another, was pulled into investigating a crime. The Amateur Sleuth might either be the victim of a crime, or he/she or any of his/her friends or relatives have been wrongfully accused. Possibly the Amateur Sleuth is confronted with the "perfect crime" - the culprit got away. Bank fraud and murder by poison fall within this category.

The Amateurs Sleuth might start a lonely investigation because of a hunch, some information the police disregards as immaterial, or - even more dramatic - because he/she is blessed (or shall we say, punished) with psychic abilities. Since most likely the Amateur Sleuth is emotionally involved in the case, he/she becomes vulnerable. The PI may have contact to police officers. The Amateur Sleuth lacks this important source of information.

Most police officers regard him/her a "whaky nincompoop." No, connections he/she "ain't got", but since the Amateur Sleuth has brain and determination, viewers will support him/her more than they will any PI or Police detective. Viewers IDENTIFY with the Amateur Sleuth. At times this subconscious identification makes even a low budget Amateur Sleuth film a box office hit.

Anyone can be pulled into solving a crime, but choosing a journalist Amateur Sleuth might be the filmmaker's best choice. Journalists have access to all kinds of information. Your doctor, teacher or insurance agent Amateur Sleuth must wade through public records.

Under the federal FOIA regulations, anyone has access to public records, unless such records violate either national security or someone's right to privacy. The following is a list of agencies the Amateur Sleuth might contact:

CITY: Traffic Court. Building Permits. Business and Professional Licenses.

COUNTY: Voter registration. Vehicle Registration. Marriage licenses and Divorce Records. Criminal Arrest. Change of Name.

FEDERAL: Military Records. Social Security Records. Bankruptcy. Immigration. Passports. Naturalization.

Most likely your Amateur Sleuth won't carry a weapon. Why not provide him/her with Maze (hairspray does an equally good job), a credit card to open locked doors - and best of all - a set of car keys to stab into the attacker's eyes. Ouch...

Once the Amateur Sleuth is ready to make contact with informants or possible suspects, he/she should TALK with them. INTERROGATION is the police detective's prerogative. TALKS are most successful if kept gossipy. And I mean GOSSIPY. "There is nothing so dangerous for anyone who has something to hide as conversation," Agatha Christie's advise still holds true. Turn you Amateur Sleuth into a busybody, have him/her react in a kindly and deeply interested way to whatever the informant (victim, witness, snitch, suspect) says. The Amateur Sleuth cajoles. More than the Police Officer and the PI he/she must read the "unsaid" by way of interpreting the informant's body language and way of speaking. Here are a few pointers:

* Does informant seems stressed (quick breathing, shoulders tense, shuffles feet).
* Does informant seem afraid (shoulders hunched, arms crossed defensively, clears throat)
* Is informant nervous (jingles change or keys, fiddles with jewelry, touches hair)
* Does informant speak in his/her normal voice, or does voice tone become either lower or high pitched (some important information remains unsaid)
* Is informant possibly personally involved, stops, repeats what has been said before, is unable to give coherent information
* If informant looks straight into the Amateur Sleuth eyes, never blinks or looks away, one can be sure he/she is either an expert liar or has been coached.

*

ACTION FILM

Action films are highly charged. The effective, audience gripping action film not only grabs the viewer's immediate attention, but keeps the viewer spellbound. Conflict is this genre's most effective selling point. Conflict is the action film's core.

The filmmaker providing ever escalating conflict adds one uncertainty after the other. All these uncertainties pose questions in dire need of answers. Yes, conflict and confrontation should be presented vividly. Only, car chases, fist fights, the God Guy shooting the Bad Guy are not the only forms of confrontation. Confrontation between a character and his/her environment, confrontation between character and fate, confrontation between a number of characters due to dissimilar believes and/or aspirations are better cores of conflict. True, these confrontations might lead to the action film's "grab-bag" of special effects and action scenes. But, and this is the important point to remember, all these action scenes must be based upon your film's main character's (protagonist's and/or antagonist's) motivation.

EXAMPLE: Bert Higgins a police captain leaves his office, a car chases him, shots are being fired. Unless we know <u>why</u> the car chase takes place, though we do enjoy the excitement on the screen, we do not get emotionally involved.

> * But if we know <u>before</u> the car chase hits us, that Ralph, Bert's old Army buddy is involved in the drug trade and tries to kill Bert we become interested.
> * We become even more interested if this sequence sets up the question, <u>who is after Bert and why.</u> Then, we not only show Exterior car chase and Interior Bert's car, but add Interior Ralph's car and dialog re. the drug trade and the planned murder.

Don't permit your action film to grow stagnant. Even intense confrontation, chases and fights grow boring if going on too long. Build up your film's conflict, via short, intense scenes, make your complications stronger, and most importantly, pay close attention to SUSPENSE. Though action, if well integrated into your film's forward movement, is your film's most sellable component, it is SUSPENSE that holds your film together:

> * Put questions into your viewer's mind. Deliver the answer. The given answer sets new questions. Or, even more exciting, the very moment when the viewer expects an answer delay the answer via action.
> * Place one or two big obstacles in your protagonist's way. Each obstacles gives rise to smaller but related obstacles before the original obstacle turns even more threatening.

Always have the viewer ask, "Why does this happen," don't have him/her wonder, "What is happening." Most importantly, never disregard the difference between ACTION and SUSPENSE:

> * ACTION, the protagonist confronts a challenge and fights (either physically or verbally)

* SUSPENSE the protagonist is not certain who or what his/her opponent is, what will be happening next, and/or whether or not he/she will overcome the obstacle.

Every event, regardless whether action or suspense dominated must lead to another logical event. It is the protagonist's (or possibly antagonist's reaction) that leads to new, even more spine tingling situations. But always remember, though action is your action film's core, never go too far astray. Always return to your plot's main story (the Main Question to be answered).

STRUCTURE is the selling SUSPENSE film's core. Before you "tackle" characterization and environment (mood), take a good look at your film's STRUCTURE:

* Has Main Conflict leading to Main Question (will A succeed in defeating B) been established clearly:
  ** Star (Main character)
  ** Opposing character's motive and goal (obstacles)
  ** Main character's motive and goal (the desire to overcome obstacles)
* Does Main Conflict tie in clearly with the leading character's motive and goal
* Does the Main Plot carry the story or has the Sub Plot taken over

The once so popular SPY THRILLER has lost its edge. Films featuring debonair heroes and gorgeous women "all creatures of a different breed", those films are past history. If you wish to revive the SPY THRILLER in some form, think about industrial or medical spying.

Why not base your action film an a true event? The film "Brubaker" - 20th Century Fox (Oscar nominated screenplay) based on the personality of Tom Morton, the prison warden who exposed secret murders in Wakefield prison, is an excellent example of the realistic action film.

*

Beginning (Act I) pulls the viewer immediately into the prison atmosphere. BRUBAKER, posing as a prisoner enters Wakefield. It is night, shadows glide and hit. Prisoners are everywhere. Faces, hands, bodies slip like ants upon the viewer. Footsteps, indistinguishable voices. TV blares, radio sounds attack.

A prisoner tortured and murdered while other prisoners, undisturbed, look on moves the story into the Middle (Act II).

Middle (Act II) Brubaker takes over as Warden. He gets to know the prisoners, not only as criminals but as human beings as well. Trying his best to improve prison conditions, he makes enemies of the local "hot shots." Worse, the moment he discovers monetary and supply thefts, high ranking Arkansas government officials are out "to get rid" of him. Strong confrontation and physical action lead from question to answer, each answer unveiling more misdeeds. Brubaker's discovery of prisoners having been murdered (Twist) leads to the Denoucment (Act III)

Denouement (Act III) The prisoners, Brubaker among them, dig up the hidden corpses. Violent action and bitter confrontations with the prison board, local and government officials lead to the film's bitter, but believable denouement - Brubaker gets fired. Nothing has changed.

*

And now a few basic guidelines:

* Hook. The star or story that brings the audience to the movie theater.
* Strong visual beginning (first three minutes)
* A central story questions (Main Question) based on either protagonist's or antagonist's goal, deals with a mystery/crime to be solved.
* Don't permit your films middle (Act II) to grow stale and static. Something must be going on all the time. Complications, obstacles, twists, surprises keep the protagonist (hero) from reaching his/her goal. Check whether Act II surprises the viewer with an exciting HIGHLIGHT scene (see segment on STRUCTURE). Rise the stakes if Act II slows down.
* Provide viewers with all the information they need.
* Questions lead to answers, answers lead to new questions.
* The protagonist must be strongly concerned about the goals set in the script.
* By defeating the antagonist (or being defeated himself/herself) the protagonist answers the Main Question and solves the mystery/crime.
* The film stops at a strong point, all "dangling threads" must be tied together.

If the plot centers on events, most likely the hero will emerge unchanged, but if the plot centers on characterization, the Protagonist undergoes a character change.

Always provide the hero with emotions the viewer will identify with, and supply him/her with something to conquer besides the obstacles the antagonist puts in the way. Permit the hero to have an emotional life, desires, dreams and aspirations, and don't forget to add some self-doubts and shortcomings. At times it is shortcomings that make a more lifelike hero.

The most effective action film leads the viewer to an intense emotional involvement not only with the hero, but with the villain as well.

Create villains that will not only frighten but fascinate and captivate the viewer. Never permit a weak antagonist to sneak across the screen. Give the antagonist reasons, deep set feeling that drive him/her to take action. The antagonist never switches MOTIVATION. Though MOTIVATION increases in strength, it is one and only one MOTIVATION that keeps the villain going.

CHARACTERIZATION/ACTION FILM

We think we know how others perceive us. We base our opinion of ourselves on our own "self concept," the person we think we are. S. J. Hayahawa explains it this way, "The primary goal of a human being is not self preservation but the preservation of the symbolic self, the self image." The goals a person sets, the actions he/she decides upon are based on self- image. Self image/concept controls all human actions. What a person wants or doesn't want depends on self concept. At times the filmmaker has to deal with a character's self concept that stands in conflict to the way others see him/her. Such a dichotomy often leads to a character's emotional conflict.

Agreed, it is the action film star's personality and most importantly <u>on screen presence</u> that dominates the action film's interpersonal relationships. Still, never "shortchange" your action film's Secondary characters. Secondary characters, who often push the plot ahead, must have a "life of their own". Stereotypes won't do. Base characterization upon each Secondary character's self image. Watching a video tape of the film "Brubaker" you will recognize the importance of Secondary characters, regardless whether friend of foe.

The action film's Secondary characters do not require the full character development necessary for the suspense drama's emotional character build up. Because of the number of Secondary characters involved in any action film, such detailed characterization would confuse the viewer. Also, don't forget, your action film MUST be build around the star, never distract from the star:

* Whose story is it? (It is the <u>star's</u>, not the antagonist's story, his/her motivation lead to goals)
* What is the story all about? (Keep the story line simple)
* Have Secondary characters <u>support </u>the star, never have them over-shadow him/her
* Bring in new plot and/or action ideas,

<u>HORROR FILM</u>

Creating a horror film takes guts.

Horror does more than superficially frighten and scare. Horror, "that thing in the shadow," digs deeply into the viewer's own, very private fears. No longer is the horror film restricted to ghosts and monsters, but films like "Silence of the Lamb" hit one with the chilling realization, "these unbelievable events on the screen could happen to me." We have to admit, horror films deal with our attraction to what we dread and fear most, the frightening eclipse of the self, this particular individual isolation that dredges fears from the subconscious. The fictionality of the events depicted on the screen permits a safe confrontation with one's personal vulnerability, it provides the valve that allows the steam of our fears to escape. Today's film-maker, therefore, needs insider knowledge of "what makes people tick." Blood and gore, once the horror film's stables won't do any longer. Blood and gore are anathema to true horror. Cruelty is no substitute for horror and even outstanding special effect, won't make a gripping horror film. In other words, don't describe fear, but <u>create</u> fear.

Horror, to be truly bone chilling, must be combined with other emotions. Don't be afraid to address complex issues. Horror is not as much about superficial shock but about the process of digging deeply into the viewer's emotional skin. This "digging" permits the viewer to chart his/her own reality in combination with the events on the screen. After all, at times we see the world, including the horror shown on the screen, not as it is, <u>but as we see it.</u> Even more challenging for the filmmaker is the bitter truth, that in some instances, horror exists beyond the grasp of the human mind.

The filmmaker creating this combination of fear and truth, fantasy and reality must take a close look at these areas:

* Plot
* Anticipation
* Mood/Environment
* Characterization

PLOT. Don't create a "layer cake" of a horror film plot where one horrific happening following the other draws the "unsuspecting, innocent" victim into paranoia's evil spider net. The monster harassing one victim after the other, until the "fearless" protagonist for unexplained reasons destroys the evil entity, is out. The bogeymen, those hitmen of days past, warning the protagonist, "Don't do this or something awful will happen to you," have gone on to their well deserved place in film history. The purpose of the effective horror film - hard to believe, but true is the creation of a specific type of communication between viewer and the event on the screen that permits paranoia to evolve due to ANTICIPATION and MOOD/ENVIRONMENT.

The monsters padding and slithering across the screen are gone, now malevolent beings are less exotic. Just take a look at Hannibal Lechter (Anthony Hopkins) "Silence of the Lambs". Doesn't he look like your neighbor, that friendly guy who goes to work every morning, moves his lawn on Saturday, attends Lion Club meetings and takes in a movie ever so often.

At times we don't even meet the killer or monster or malevolent force. In life, aren't we at times scarred of unseen events or situations we know do exist, but are unable to define...You see, today's filmmakers have expanded the horror film's boundaries. Films like "Silence of the Lamb" accept that evil not only exists, but is difficult - if not impossible - to overcome. The effective horror film of today dealing with this hidden fear of the unexplained hovering all around us depends upon ANTICIPATION.

ANTICIPATION

Anticipation of a horrific event is far more suspenseful than the event itself. After all, shadows are more frightening than the real thing. Anticipation deals with human emotions. It is the uneasy acceptance of fear and emotions that separates the memorable horror film from the mediocre one. The filmmaker, therefore, must ask himself/herself, "What do I want the viewer to feel? How do I want him/her to feel? And what are the details I need to convey a very specific emotion and/or fear."

Remember, anticipation/suspense results somewhat less from the viewer's identification with the protagonist but his/her identification with the horrific event the protagonist faces. DELAYING the horrific event gives the viewer the feeling of falling through space. The filmmaker uses the elements of mood (lighting, sound) and pacing (intensity levels) as he/she creates the desired, and at times difficult to achieve, anticipation levels. The following examples (based on the film FROZEN SCREAM) suggest effective ways to handle the difficult task of creating anticipation:

Example I	* Build up anticipation slowly - slowly - and more slowly before delivering the event (discovering Tom dead).
Example II	* Built up anticipation, but don't deliver the event, (discovering Tom dead),
Example III	* Build up anticipation, then deliver the event differently from what the viewer expected.

Anticipation is the filmmaker's safeguard if he/she works on a "run of the mill," humdrum horror scene such as this:

Anne afraid that something dreadful has happened to her husband, enters their home.

Example I.   * Build up anticipation slowly - slowly - slowly before delivering the event.

Use light patterns to build up anticipation.

EXTERIOR VICTORIAN MANSION. NIGHT.
Dim moonlight filters across a square Victorian building. On ANNE exciting her car. Slowly, ever so slowly, her eyes on the house, she walks across the front yard.

ANNE's POV. The moonlit mansion.

Back on ANNE. She hesitates for a moment. At the front door, again she hesitates before she turns the doorknob and opens the door.

INTERIOR VICTORIAN MANSION NIGHT. HALLWAY
ANNE enters. The hallway, a dark cavern, looms.

                              ANNE
                    Tom....
There is no answer.

ANNE fumbles for the light switch. The hallway remains steeped in darkness. ANNE makes her way to the staircase. Moonlight streaks across the stairs.

INTERIOR VICTORIAN MANSION NIGHT. STAIRCASE
ANNE, her hand on the bannister, moves up the stairs. Moonlight and dark shadows swirl over the walls. And now a warning, the deep sounds of a grandfather clock striking three, swings through the night. For a moment ANNE stops at the landing, she listens.

                              ANNE
                    Tom...

And again no answer. Anne, even slower now, moves up the staircase.

INTERIOR VICTORIAN MANSION. NIGHT. UPPER HALLWAY
Holding on to the wall ANNE moves along the hallway. She stops at a partially open door. Pushes it open and enters.

INTERIOR VICTORIAN MANSION. NIGHT. STUDY.
Moonlight floods the room. ANNE looks around.

ANNE's POV. A paper littered desk, a turned over chair.

Back on ANNE, she leaves.

INTERIOR VICTORIAN MANSION. NIGHT. UPPER HALLWAY.
Again ANNE hesitates, but then she forces herself to open another door. Still standing in the hallway, she reaches for the light switch.

13

INTERIOR VICTORIAN MANSION. NIGHT. BEDROOM.

ANNE's POV. A bedroom. Light flooded

SHOCK ZOOM. TOM sprawls on the bed, his shirt is half open, blood covering his chest, seeps onto the bedspread. Electrodes protrude from his forehead. His eyes stare.

Back on ANNE a silent scream.

> VO. VOICE (whispering)
> The angels are here.

Hands - almost a caress - slide up ANNE's arms.

Frozen, slowly - ever so slowly - ANNE turns her head.

ANNE's POV. Barely visible against the dark hallway a black hooded figure looms behind her,

Back on ANNE. Black gloved hands clamp around her throat.

Example II. Build up anticipation, but don't deliver the event. Scenes move on a faster pace. Sound builds up fear.

EXTERIOR VICTORIAN MANSION. NIGHT.
Thunder rolls, lightening flashes, rain pounds upon a square Victorian building.

On ANNE exiting her car, she hurries across the front yard, runs up a few steps, throws the front door open and enters the house.

INTERIOR VICTORIAN MANSION. NIGHT. HALLWAY.
Her voice almost drowned by thunder, ANNE yells

> ANNE
> Tom...

There is no answer.

> ANNE
> Tom...

Fumbling through her purse ANNE pulls out a flashlight. The dim stream of light wavering in front of her, she rushes to the staircase.

INTERIOR VICTORIAN MANSION. NIGHT. STAIRCASE.
ANNE hurries up the staircase. Her flashlight wavers, lighting flashes, thunder rolls, rain pours down.

INTERIOR VICTORIAN MANSION. NIGHT. UPPER HALLWAY.
ANNE, almost falling, stumbles to a door. Throws it open. The sound of thunder grows louder.

<u>INTERIOR VICTORIAN MANSION. NIGHT. STUDY.</u>
A flash of light across a paper littered desk. Then - darkness.

ON ANNE huddling against the door.

ANNE's POV, her flashlight wavers over some upturned chairs. Books litter the floor.

Back on ANNE she turns.

<u>INTERIOR VICTORIAN MANSION. NIGHT. UPPER HALLWAY.</u>
ANNE moves on to the next door, she opens it.

<u>INTERIOR VICTORIAN MANSION. NIGHT. BEDROOM.</u>
By now thunder threatens from far away, lightening has grown weaker, but the rain still pounds. ANNE walks through the room. She looks at the bed, opens the closet, opens the bathroom door, calls out softly -

ANNE

Tom...

And now, unexpectedly, another blast of thunder, again lightening strikes. ANNE hurries from the room.

<u>INTERIOR VICTORIAN MANSION. NIGHT. UPPER HALLWAY</u>
ANNE hurries through the hallway to the staircase.

<u>INTERIOR VICTORIAN MANSION. NIGHT. STAIRCASE</u>
On ANNE running down the stairs.

<u>INTERIOR VICTORIAN MANSION. NIGHT. HALLWAY</u>
ANNE runs to the door. She reaches for the door handle when a voice groans -

VO. VOICE

The angels are here...

PULL IN on ANNE as hands clamp around her throat.

<u>Example III.</u> Build up anticipation, then deliver event differently from what the viewer had expected.

Same as <u>Example # II</u> including ANNE running down the staircase, before we continue:

<u>INTERIOR VICTORIAN MANSION. NIGHT. HALLWAY.</u>
ANNE rushes through the hallway and out the door.

<u>EXTERIOR VICTORIAN MANSION. NIGHT.</u>
Again thunder rolls, lightening flashes and rain pounds as ANNE runs to her car.

INTERIOR ANNE's CAR. NIGHT.
Gasping ANNE pulls out her car keys, starts her car, and steps on the gas. Backing out, ANNE turns her head -

POV ANNE A streak of lightening reveals TOM slumped on the back seat. Blood covers his shirt, electrodes protrude from his head.

And now a voice -

                              VO. VOICE
                    The angel's are here...

ENVIRONMENT
Environment provides the emotional window to very specific moments. Horror measured by environment is truly frightening.
        Strange as it may sound, to make a horror film gripping, environment does not refer to some place in fantasyland, but is firmly grounded in stark reality. Don't be vague but be specific and do relay heavily on telling detail. The emotional atmosphere, based on mood, setting and subtly expanding detail, silently but efficiently explains plot and characters.
        Take a look at the following three examples, and notice how environment and mood change the scenic moment. This is the scene:
        A room at night. The protagonist, awake, fears for his/her life as someone enters the room.

Environment I. A concentration camp's dormitory.

INTERIOR DORMITORY. NIGHT.
Shadows cut across rows of cots lined up against the wall. PULL IN on ROBERT. ROBERT, his body rigid, lays on one of the cots. Footsteps - boots clicking on a stone floor - approach. ROBERT remains motionless. The sound of a door opening makes him look up.

Pull in tighter on ROBERT as a flood of harsh light washes over him.

ROBERT'S POV. Two guards, ready to march people to the gas chamber, enter the room. One of the guards pauses in front of ROBERT, looks at him.

On ROBERT. ROBERT locks eyes with the guard.

Environment II. The dormitory of a Victorian Finishing School.

INTERIOR DORMITORY. NIGHT.
The room lays steeped in shadows. The yellow light from a gas lantern located somewhat down the street wavers across one of the beds where RITA, eyes wide open, huddles under the covers.

RITA's POV. The door opens a crack.

Back on RITA shaking with fear.

RITA's POV. The door opens. A dark shadow slides in.

On RITA, motionless. The shadows hovering over the room, move in on her.

Environment III A suburban bedroom.

INTERIOR BEDROOM. NIGHT.
The light of a small lamp glowing on the night stand wraps the room in soft light. ANGIE talks on the phone. Suddenly, listening to footsteps coming up the stairs, her body grows tense. She throws down the receiver, reaches for her robe while the footsteps, louder and faster now, move up the hallway. ANGIE runs to the window. And now -slowly ever so slowly - the sound of a door opening. Frantically ANGIE tries to open the window. The window remains closed. A shot. ANGIE crumbles to the floor.

Angie's POV. The barrel of a gun pointed at her.

*

Light and sound, as demonstrated by above three examples, play an important part in the creation of mood and environment as the filmmaker pays close attention to:

* Light source, light intensity
* Sound, sound intensity

Characters reaction and/or conception of light and sound is most important.
Take some time to compare the bone chilling environment of example I, the eery strangeness of environment of example II to the everyday environment of example III.
The familiarity of the everyday environment worked well for two classic films, "Exorcist" and "Poltergeist". In both film it is the everyday world so familiar to the viewer, that turns frightening as soon as horror takes over. The moment the extraordinary invades, the environment changes slowly and bit by bit. This is when accurate detail comes in. Subtly expanding detail clarifies to the viewer the situation on hand and the involved characters perception of it. In "Poltergeist" the involved characters perception of their home and their relationship to one another changes as soon as the supernatural invades. In "Exorcist" the evil makes itself known by stressing the change in seemingly unimportant visual details. Translated into "film-language" we understand that in "Poltergeist" the viewer is shown the characters' perception of their environment, while in "Exorcist" the supernatural evil attacks the viewer.

Light and sound show a character's reaction to a given situation, but it is camera angles and editing that shows the changed environment. Here dynamic camera angles and editing and emphatic camera angles and editing gain importance. Let's take a look at the following scene:

Allen enters his deceased grandfather's living room. He looks at his grandfather's portrait threatening above the mantel.

Dynamic Camera Angle and Editing. Dynamic camera angles and editing creates the viewer's emotional reaction.

<u>LIVING ROOM. DAY.</u>
ALLEN enters. He walks to the desk and puts down his briefcase.

Pull in on ALLEN. TILTED CAMERA (Camera angle) the walls seem to fall upon him.

ALLEN takes a deep breath, the moment he shakes his head (quick cut editing) the room returns to normal. He looks up -

ALLEN's POV. His grandfather's stern portrait above the mantel.

<u>Empathic Camera Angle and Editing.</u> Empathic camera angles and editing shows the <u>character's</u> emotional condition.

<u>LIVING ROOM DAY.</u>
ALLEN enters. He walks to the desk and puts down his briefcase.

PULL IN on ALLEN as he looks up, and after a short hesitation walks to his grandfather's portrait hanging over the mantel.

Allen's POV. ZOOM (short cut editing) to portrait as his grandfather portrait seems to attack ALLEN

Back on ALLEN,(short cut editing). Dazed he stares at the portrait.

<u>CHARACTERIZATION</u>
Stereotypes have no place in any horror film. The characters on the screen, their actions, their ways of expression, their beliefs, fears and aspirations as well as their relationship to one another, only will grip the viewer if these are based on true (either good or evil) emotions. This emotional panoply is missing in most of the run of the mill "entertaining" horror films. The characters on the screen should not only deal with the problem inherent in the horror situation but - granted on a secondary emotional level (subplot) - with another problem as well.

Creating the horror film's characters is not as easy as it seems: Make your characters believable and true to life, but avoid the complexity of characterization necessary to make the dramatic suspense film believable.

The horror film deals with two character categories, the everyday protagonist and the antagonist who operating on a "different emotional, intellectual and psychological level", is either human, supernatural, ghostly, or has invaded the protagonist's mind . First let's take a look at the Antagonist.

<u>ANTAGONIST</u>
The antagonist makes your horror film gripping. The truth is, it is the antagonist, not the protagonist, who truly creates your horror film. Play the antagonist against the protagonist's personality. Each incident pushing the horror film ahead, must suggest and/or reveal something about the antagonist's distorted emotional, psychologically criminal or possibly supernatural make up. This means every event/situation pushing the horror film's plot ahead must be instigated by this specific person or superhuman entity - the antagonist.

Don't ever be satisfied with the stereotypical antagonist, but create a being - human, inhuman, or supernatural including the proverbial ghost - who is "drawn by something" out of the ordinary. "Silence of the Lamb" provides an excellent example how a twisted emotional core turned a man into a monster.

Nothing in Hannibal Lechter's behavior makes the viewer suspect a psycho-killer, but the viewer senses the evil animating from this character, and gets chilled. In "Exorcist" we watch a likable young girl, turn into a supernatural, truly inhuman monster. "Exorcist", in a fascinating way, combines victim and Antagonist within one person, the possessed child.

Introducing the antagonist the filmmaker has these choices:

* Spring the antagonist upon your unsuspecting viewer.
* Show the antagonist from the very beginning as the evil element or the inhuman force he/she is.
* Introduce a supposedly evil element and/or person, then reveal the true antagonist.
* Introduce a very likable person, and slowly reveal the antagonist he/she is.

PROTAGONIST

Never permit the Protagonist to either overshadow your film's horror situation, or to overtake your film's concept. The protagonist <u>contributes</u> to the situation, but he/she doesn't <u>control</u> it. The control, until defeated (or victorious) lies with the evil force. Not an easy job, believe you me. Always keep in mind:

* Avoid a passive protagonist (one of the major flaws of the run of the mill horror film.)
* Do not have your protagonist act irrationally, but let him/her make logical decisions.
* The time when the protagonist' innocent (let's admit it, dumb character) controlled the film's basic idea, these times are gone.

Creating the horror film protagonists is far different from creating a protagonist for the "who done it" action or dramatic suspense film. Suspense drama, "who done it" and action films portray protagonists realistically. The effective horror film in contrast exploits some anomaly, something that is different, possibly wrong, within the Protagonist's realistic emotional make-up. Viewing the protagonist in this light, the protagonist's emotions and actions become inseparable from setting and mood as his/her emotions intertwine and/or collide with the antagonist's goal. This vague but nevertheless existing relationship between Protagonist and Antagonist demands that the Protagonist's reaction to events, other characters and situation, <u>must be shown clearly</u>.

DIALOG

Keep dialog clear, short and relevant to the character portrayed. Everyday speech patterns, as in all SUSPENSE films are your best choice. "Other worldly" sounding dialog is out.

*

SUSPENSE DRAMA

Today's suspense drama reflects an uncompromising realism that delves deeply into a character's psychological makeup. The suspense drama's protagonist, antagonist and the plot's Main Question are not as clearly defined as in any other SUSPENSE film, since it is PREMISE that ties the plot together. PREMISE is the hidden story, the undercurrent beneath the suspense drama's plot. PREMISE has little to do with either the featured characters motives, goals and actions. PREMISE does not answer the Main Question, but it deals with the question the FILMMAKER WANTS TO ASK.

Two films, "IMMORTAL BELOVED" and "WAR OF THE ROSES" provide clear examples of PREMISE.

* "IMMORTAL BELOVED - lets the viewer discover Beethoven's twisted personality, as the executor of Beethoven's will searches for Beethoven's Immortal Beloved. PREMISE QUESTION: Was Beethoven, because of his genius, above moral obligations and restrictions. MAIN QUESTION: Will the Executor of Beethoven's will find the Immortal Beloved.
* "WAR OF ROSES" subjects the viewer to the apex of materialism, as fighting each other for the possession of their home, both, husband and wife die. PREMISE QUESTION: Are we caught up in materialism? MAIN QUESTION: Who will keep the house?

Within the first ten minutes of screen time, the suspense drama establishes the environment's sights and sounds, regardless whether happy, sinister or "every day" boring. "Immortal Beloved" gives an excellent example of the integration of environment (19th Century Vienna), mood, music, story context and verbally unexpressed but deeply felt emotions.

At times if you set up the ending in the beginning (as shown in "War of Roses," both protagonists meet at an auction and bid for the same painting) you'll give a glimpse of things to come. Act I establishes the couple's competitive personalities, and as such foreshadows a competition that will eventually lead to their death.

Make your beginning interesting but don't overload it. Don't have the viewer "digest" too much. Don't forget you'll have a long Middle (ACT II) to work on. While the "who done it", the horror and the action film lend themselves to exiting and surprising plot developments, the suspense drama's Act II often grows stagnant and therefore boring. So, what should you do?

* Begin Act II with a dramatic scene
* Either create new emotional, mental or relationship problems, or intensify the ones originated in Act I.
* Whenever the viewer expects the solution of problem, delay the solution ("War of the Roses")
* Provide options - what to do and not to do - for your film's characters ("War of Roses")
* All scenes, though different in story line, must be plot-connected ("Immortal Beloved)
* Not all scenes have to be emotionally charged, at times restrained behavior is more effective.

The "who done it," and the action film depend on the Subjective View Point (events seen from the Protagonist's point of view), while the suspense drama stresses the Shifting Viewpoint (events as seen from a number of characters point of view.) Shifting Viewpoint, usually deals with two different plots, both based on two strong, individual core stories. These two plots (same as Main Plot and Sub Plot) MUST converge at various points, as demonstrated in "Immortal Beloved". But go easy. Shifting Viewpoint, unless handled skillfully, might confuse viewers. At times the traditional Main Plot and Sub Plot structure will be a better choice.

EMOTIONS ARE THE SUSPENSE DRAMA'S LIFE BLOOD

Characters are the suspense drama's backbone. While basic, though careful characterization will serve all areas of the "who done it" and the horror film, while a character's self-concept is the action's film key, the suspense drama's characterization must reach deeper into the human mind and soul.

Observing, understanding and possibly supporting a character's emotions the viewer forms a symbiotic relationship with the character on the screen. Since this relationship is based on specifics, the filmmaker must find ways to express emotions visually. The novelist and the dramatist have it much easier. The novelist expresses a character's feelings and thoughts via INNER MONOLOG. No one worries if characters on stage express their feelings verbally. The filmmaker, however, not only expresses characters emotions visually and verbally, but the emotions expressed and shown must be real, never contrived:

* Express character's emotional layers vividly and specifically.
* Show how characters perceive events, situations and relationships. Show how they think and feel.
* Yes, show characters one loves to hate.
* Fools, dreamers and rouges make strong antiheroes. But don't make him/her a passive bystander.

Regardless of your on screen character's intellectual state of mind it is EMOTION that carries the viewer affective suspense drama. Remember the viewer SEES, the viewer FEELS, its as simple as that.

* Viewer OBSERVES character on screen
* Viewer RECOGNIZES EMOTIONS EXPRESSED
* Viewer SUPPORTS THESE EMOTIONS
* Viewer EXPERIENCES the emotions the character experiences

Emotions are a state of mind. Before you start exploring any given emotion make certain the viewer knows what CAUSED this particular emotion (remember, CAUSE and EFFECT). The answer will help you to zoom in on a SPECIFIC emotion. Take ANGER for instance. Never try to express ANGER generally, but explore WHAT KIND OF ANGER the character on screen experiences. Is it rage, frustration, shame of even apathy?

Though on-screen expression of emotions can be handled in many different ways, emotions must be expressed CLEARLY:

* Express emotions visually
  ** Actors performances
  ** Handling of props

      ** Physical actions
    * Express emotions cinematographically
      ** Mood (environment, light plot, sound)
      ** Camera angles and moves, editing

EXCITEMENT may either be a positive or negative emotion. Choose exclamations and short sentences, a well as staccato physical movements and handling of props.

Positive Excitement Peggy and Bill go on a cruise

PEGGY
Got everything ready.

BILL
Airline tickets - passports

PEGGY
In my purse

Negative Excitement Peggy and Bill caught in an earthquake

PEGGY
Let's get out of here

BILL
Got to grab my documents

PEGGY
Come on - - no - - here it goes again

SHAME Decide whether you are expressing SHAME, SURPRISE or UNCERTAINTY. If expressed verbally, these emotions require a disconnected speech pattern:

WALTER
I always told you, I'd - - But- - What did you say? Yes - - I saw Emelie, - - right - - about the document, I meant to tell you - -

ANGER Apply GOALS (what a character wants to achieve) and INTENSITY LEVELS (how strongly a character express himself/herself, please take a look at the DIALOG chapter) as you move actors through a HATE/ANGER scene. Use ATTITUDE if you wish to add some "salt and pepper"

AL's goal: I want to NETTLE
Ervin's goal: I want to INFURIATE

ERVIN
And because of your incompetence we'll...

> AL
> Incompetence? Please explain. Don't hold back.

> ERVIN
> Here we go again. Let me tell you...you don't know everything.

> AL
> Really? I guess I've forgotten more than you ever knew about raising pedigreed pups.

GRIEF, APATHY Decide upon the precise emotion you wish to express. Setting (mood, light) is your most powerful tool. Verbal expression is laconic, physical actions are subdued. If any possible, add appropriate sound.

Rosa's Living Room. Night (Grief)
The room is steeped in darkness. Rosa reaches for Henry's photo. (Light plot)

Rosa's Living Room. Day (Apathy)
Rosa crouches in a chair. Slowly she gets up. Laboriously she walks to the desk and reaches for Henry's photo. (Physical action)

Rosa's Office. Day (Apathy)
Motionless Rosa sits at her desk. Rain splatters against the window. Telephones shrill. Voices are all around her (Sound)

LONELINESS, LONGING An overcast day. Shrubs and trees have turned into gray shadows (light plot). Minimum dialog.

FEAR. Fear might either result in frantic physical actions or spine freezing terror. Again setting and light plots combined with sound effects are the answer to scenes of high fear. Thunder rolls, rain splashes, lightening strikes through a room. Or, showing spine tingling fear, have sounds come closer and closer.

CONTENTMENT, HAPPINESS. Sunshine turning a meadow into gold, moonshine shimmering on water, a comfortable room illuminated by soft light, all these light effects spell contentment and happiness.

ANXIETY Dialog moves in a frantic pace, short sentences and exclamations. Harsh light gives the viewer the visual aspect of ANXIETY, while sound effects such as traffic sounds, whirring machines, loud music, voices shouting and babbling off-screen, intensify the feeling of uneasiness.

DESPAIR. Despair, depending upon the situation, might fall into the emotional range of either GRIEF or ANXIETY. Depending on the story line it might be a combination of both. Setting (mood) any sound effects have to be adjusted carefully.

*

PART II

THE REALITY OF THE MOMENT

PLOT STRUCTURE MADE EASY

Plot structure is the road map that leads to a gripping Suspense film:

* Act I, a crime (or incident) happens. Introduce hero, possibly villain and state the Main Question.
* Act II provides the obstacles that keep hero from reaching his/her goal. First introduce, then eliminate some suspects.
* Act III reveals main culprit and provides the solution.

ACT I, ACT II and ACT III deal with the following structural details:

MOTIVE. MOTIVE provides the hero with the reason TO DO SOMETHING about a situation. His/her decision leads to GOALS resulting in ACTION. A MOTIVE is based on the villain's NEED to throw an obstacle into the hero's way, and on the hero's NEED to overcome the obstacle. The plot must provide both hero (protagonist) and villain (antagonist) with MOTIVE (Why I want to do something), MEANS (How I will do something) and OPPORTUNITY (when I want to do something). Considering the hero's and/or villain's reaction to a given motivation, ask yourself, "Why would the character do this." (MOTIVE) and, "How would the character do this." (GOAL).

NEEDS are based and AFFINITY (the desire to hold on) or REPULSION (the desire to eliminate).

INFORMATION The hero is after INFORMATION, and because of the received INFORMATION he/she poses a questions that in turn leads to new INFORMATION. Act II provides this question-answer cycle. Unless a character has received INFORMATION he/she cannot take action. Feed in INFORMATION carefully, too much information at any given time will confuse viewers. Repeat important INFORMATION three times. The first time the viewer disregards it, the second time the viewer might remember, the third time "the message sinks in." Provide false information (RED HERRING). Make this MISINFORMATION (clue) important.

GOAL A GOAL is based on a character's decision to overcome (positive GOAL) something, or (negative GOAL) to avoid/prevent something. If a GOAL is both positive and negative, you fail to present a clear dramatic situation. You might, however, show a character struggling with the problem which Goal to choose.

MAIN QUESTION Every SUSPENSE film needs to be constructed upon one MAIN QUESTION (Main Plot) leading to MAIN GOAL and an additional SUB-QUESTION leading to SUB-GOALS (Sub Plot). The film's denouement answers both MAIN QUESTION AND SUB QUESTION. Take a look at the attached script and you will notice:

24

* MAIN QUESTION (Main Plot) - Why was Tom killed?
* SUB QUESTION (Sub Plot) - Will Anne and Kevin be happy
together?

PROBLEM A PROBLEM must increase in strength and importance. It must have "staying power". Don't have the hero solve the problem at the middle of Act II and add a second PROBLEM. Adding a new and different PROBLEM will rip the plot apart. In all SUSPENSE films, excepting Police Procedures and PI plots, the PROBLEM has to affect the hero or someone close to him/her.

CONFLICT/OBSTACLES are your SUSPENSE film's life blood. CONFLICT needs to be based on the way characters view each other and the world around them. CONFLICT may be subtle or overt, but always states clearly who is set against WHOM or WHAT. Don't relay on the CONFLICT situation only, but always show character's reaction to the event. Always point out the consequences if hero doesn't overcome the OBSTACLE. Clarify the motivation behind the OBSTACLE. OBSTACLE must rise in severity or your film has no dramatic value. Forget about benevolent coincidences. The Hero's determination overcomes the OBSTACLES. Most OBSTACLES are planned, a few, called COMPLICATIONS, are of accidental nature. COMPLICATIONS must evolve from the given OBSTACLE.

SUSPENSE is your films most important effect. SUSPENSE requires a strong anticipation buildup. Don't ever consider that withholding INFORMATION will add to suspense. On the contrary, withholding information confuses the viewer. Keep the viewer in suspense, work on anticipation and make certain events will happen though not necessarily the way when or how the viewer had anticipated.
     Another effect of anticipation is delay. Have the viewer expect something to happen, but time passes by. Then, when the viewer at least expects it, the dreaded event occurs.
     SUSPENSE is doubt. The forces of success or failure must be equal. If these forces are unequal we have no suspense.
     Overlapping SUSPENSE. Make certain that each of the viewers questions, "what will happen next?" will be answered. But "overlap" answers and new questions. Think of SUSPENSE as a coil of rope. Pull it tighter and tighter.

SURPRISE. SURPRISE, the viewer expects an event but nothing or a different event occurs.

TWIST. Twist must be strong enough to create a character's need to overcome a threatening situation. TWIST at the end of Act I sets the story in motion.

CLUES The viewer needs clues to understand the way the hero tries to overcome his/her problem. At times it helps to place either a clue or a question leading to a clue at the end of a scene. A CLUE might be an event that raises a question, or a physical CLUE such as a piece of clothing, a letter, etc. Via CLUES give the viewer hope then take the hope away.

CLIFF HANGERS (when everything seems lost) should not happen accidentally, but must be a legitimate part of the plot.

ACT I

Act I sets up the information of WHERE - WHO - WHY and asks the MAIN QUESTION. The opening of Act I not only sets your film's atmosphere but establishes the viewer's curiosity. A slow, psychological oriented opening might be perfect for your horror film or suspense drama, but it won't do for an action film. But regardless of your film's genre you'll have to HOOK the viewer from the very beginning. Distributors, keep in mind, look at the first few minutes of Act I as they decide to pass on a film immediately or to keep on watching. For this very reason your beginning must be strong visually as well as emotionally. Start your film with either:

* Visual HOOK (atmosphere or action)
* Puzzling event
* Verbal argument

Regardless whether you have decided upon a slow or fast opening, Act I must feature the following:
* Scene I sets a problem
* Scene II adds suspense
* Scene III provides a short lull (give additional information about characters, environment and/or back story)
* End of Act I, unexpectedly, WHAM-BANG supplies the TWIST and sets up the MAIN QUESTION.
* TWIST might be based upon a previous incident, or an event happening at present.
** TWIST sets up the PROBLEM, it is the instigating factor for all obstacles and conflicts dealt with in Act II
** There must be a logical connection (cause and effect) between the TWIST and plot development
** TWIST puts the hero in jeopardy

Act II

All through Act II the plot "thickens" as opposing forces are pitted against each other. Now is the time to develop characters and their relationships and, if necessary, change emotions and relationships. Act II brings in a Sub Plot, or Sub-Plots that, intersecting with the Main Plot, will answer the MAIN QUESTION in Act III.

At best, beginning of Act II is on a lower level than ending (Twist) of Act I.

Every scene must move the story forward (forward movement, based on cause and effect). Do not permit action to overshadow the plot. Don't let dialog slow down your film. If exposition (background information and or/explanation) is necessary, make these scenes visually interesting.

Avoid rambling or loosely connected scenes. Every scene must have a purpose based on either heroes or villains NEED.

Something must have changed at the end of every scene. A question may have been answered, a new question may have been set. There might a surprise, a minor TWIST, a strengthening of OBSTACLE/CONFLICT or even a small victory.

Act II pits opposing forces against each other. Strengthen obstacles and conflicts, but avoid repetitions, unrelated episodes and coincidences.

Set up sufficient clues. Some of these clues might be RED HERRINGS.

Create a number of PIVOTAL scenes, scenes illuminating what is most important in the plot.

After a high intensity scene, bring in a PACE-BREAKER, a scene of lower intensity as to give the viewer the chance "to take a breath."

Act II makes the villain's motive more fascinating, logical and believable.

For the middle of Act II, when things threaten to slow down create a HIGHLIGHT SCENE. This scene is a gripping PIVOTAL scene, a short drama featuring a beginning, middle and end.

Toward middle of Act II and at the end of Act II state your film's MAIN QUESTION again.

An element of strong anticipation is mandatory as OBSTACLE, CONFLICT and COMPLICATIONS increase.

Provide a short lull before events move to your film's CLIMAX. CLIMAX refers to the plot's DARK MOMENT, when everything seems lost. CLIMAX leads to another TWIST. This TWIST, stronger than the one occurring at the end of Act I, leads into Act III.

Act III

Act III has a beginning, a middle and an end. Remain within the framework of CAUSE and EFFECT. The antagonistic forces grow more challenging. Hero faces insurmountable OBSTACLES. The villain's strength, forcing the hero into significant decisions, leads to DENOUEMENT.

The DENOUEMENT, features three parts:

Before solution is reached (I)
Solution in progress   (II)
Solution, hero either wins or looses (III)

Lead up to Solution during I. Answer MAIN Question(WHO committed the crime, and WHY or HOW was crime committed) and all questions relating to Main- Plot and Sub-Plot, tie up all "dangling threats" during II. Hit the viewer with the plot's Solution in III.

NITTY-GRITTY BUT IMPORTANT
Before you get ready to shoot your film, give the script a thorough "once-over" by answering these questions:

* Who are the characters featured, and how are they involved in the event (situation)
* Does Cause and Effect:
  ** give new information (answers)
  ** move the story forward
  ** answer previous questions
* Conflict strengthened throughout plot

* Where does event (situation) take place, is environment important to character and/or plot development
* Does something specific happen in each scene, or is the scene a rehash of previous events.
* Scene drags - cut it and telescope dialog
* Motivation weak - make it stronger
* Check for CAUSE and EFFECT progression
* Are there enough SUSPENSE questions and have questions been answered
* Do all characters sound alike? Adjust dialog.
* Rewrite dialog if:
  ** Overwritten
  ** Does not reveal character
  ** Cliche
* Are characters diversified enough
* Is ANTAGONIST too weak or uninteresting
* Are obstacles unclear, or too easily overcome

VIEWPOINT.

Remember, the success of any film depends upon the partnership of the viewer and the story told on the screen. This partnership is based upon VIEWPOINT.

VIEWPOINT refers to what is shown on the screen while POV (Point of View) refers to what a characters sees. The filmmaker has to consider these VIEWPOINTS:

* OBJECTIVE VIEWPOINT, facts are shown in a straight forward way.
* SUBJECTIVE VIEWPOINT, everything is seen from the hero's viewpoint. This viewpoint, placing the viewer into the hero's shoes, results in strong viewer identification.
* OMNIPOTENT VIEWPOINT, The viewer is fully aware of both the hero's and the villain's intentions and actions. At times this viewpoint adds to SUSPENSE, other times it may obstruct the story line.
* MULTIPLE VIEWPOINT refers to OMNIPOTENT VIEW-POINT involving several people. MULTIPLE VIEWPOINT is most effective for comedic situations or scenes of intense verbal confrontation
  ** Character 1 has a goal
  ** Character 2 has an opposing goal
  ** Character 3 keeps character 1 from achieving goal
  ** Character 4 complicates situation

CHARACTERIZATION MADE EASY

The viewer must have curiosity about the characters on the screen. Melodramatic, cliche situations and emotions are not the key to the viewer's empathy. Unless the filmmaker shows what characters feel and do, explains the reasons for their actions, and explores their relationship to other characters, the filmmaker is not doing his/her job.

Dialog alone does not describe a characters sufficiently. It is BEHAVIOR based on the under-laying character core that makes the viewer relate to the characters on the screen.

Never create bland characters, the typical housewife, typical cop, typical college student. Beware of the so called "everyday, ordinary" people. Such people do not exist. Not one of is ordinary we all have characteristics and attitudes of our own. Emotional interchange between characters must be dynamic. This doesn't mean characters have to shout at each other. Emotions are equally effective is suppressed. Always be aware of the attraction and/or repulsion element present in every relationship.

This segment focuses on these CHARACTERIZATION "tools":

> * Traits
> > ** Flat Character
> > ** Simple Character
> > ** Complex Character
> * Emotional Arc
> > ** Need

Always base your characters emotional parameters upon differences in ATTITUDE, TEMPERAMENT and REFERENCE.

As day by day fictitious characters flit across our TV screens, the filmmaker, inadvertently, basing his/her SUSPENSE film's characterizations upon these interpretations may end up with "just another bunch" of cliches. My advice is to find out WHY a character reacts in specific ways to events and people. By exploring character TRAITS the filmmaker will find the answer to the WHY.

Concentrating on TRAITS is not only an easier way to get the difficult and often frustrating job of characterization done, but leads to more diversification between both, opposing and supporting characters. (Remember, the script supplies you with a character's dialog but leaves characterization up to you). TRAITS can be positive, negative or a combination of both:

> * Positive TRAITS (kindness, warmth, caring moral values,
> etc.)
> * Negative TRAITS (selfishness, cruelty, deviousness, etc.)

The filmmaker deals with these character categories:

Flat Character This character has no recognizable TRAITS, but shows ATTITUDE or BEHAVIOR. Day players such as a waiter, taxi driver, doorman, secretary, usually are Flat Characters.

Simple Character This character has one outstanding character TRAIT. This TRAIT might either be positive or negative, but never the combination of both. Since most action films feature a Simple Characters Star do not change the Star from a Simple Character to a Complex Character, unless this change has been foreshadowed and is necessary for plot development.

Surround the Star with colorful and interesting supporting characters (possibly one or two Complex Characters) but DO NOT overshadow the Simple Character Star. Supporting characters are important for any film. They move the plot ahead by providing background information and exposition, but their purpose is to support the Star, not to overshadow him/her.

<u>Complex Character</u> The Complex Character shows two TRAITS. Combine the basic character TRAIT with either a complimentary or opposing TRAIT.

> * Complimentary TRAITS. A positive TRAIT (kindness) is strength-
> ened by a second positive TRAIT (consideration).
> * Opposing TRAITS. A positive TRAIT (warmth) is countered by a
> negative TRAIT (deviousness)

TRAITS are especially important for the character driven suspense drama where events are based upon, and must result from the plot's main characters TRAITS.

In the character driven SUSPENSE film featuring a plot that depends more on character than events, the filmmaker has to deal with the EMOTIONAL ARC, the emotional change a character undergoes. This ARC might focus on either mental, emotional or behavioral change caused by:

> * Change of environment and/or relationship
> * Character's subconscious need for change
> * The way others treat a character

The EMOTIONAL ARC might bring to light some either beneficial or less beneficial aspects of a character's behavior and attitude. These changes might cause a plot's TWIST, a SURPRISE or even reversal of events. But never confront the unsuspecting viewer with any behavioral or relationship change unless this change has been foreshadowed.

External problems may cause INNER CONFLICT The <u>voice of passion</u>, Leila has had it with her boring life, she wants to "kiss her job good-by", move to New York or Hollywood and "go into acting", but the <u>voice of reason</u> makes her realize she, a single mother, needs her humdrum job to support her child.

At times your plot might be based on a past event, that affected hero or villain, or possibly both. This is where NEED, a subconscious drive, plays an important role. In most cases NEED arises from a person's low self esteem. The affected person, however, is unaware of his/her driving NEED force.

> * Billy's family was poor:
> ** William Hamlyn, Vice-President of Whatever Incorporated, though
> stingy with wife and children, has made money his sacred cow.
> (NEED: I have to hold on to money).
> ** William Hamlyn the motion picture executive likes to show off. By
> now he has married his third "trophy wife", his mansion is one of Beverly
> Hill's show places.
> (NEED: I've to show I've got it).
> ** William Hamlyn, the unemployed welder abuses his wife and children.
> (NEED: I have to punish others for the deprivation I once suffered).

> * Billy, the small child, never received the love and attention he not only craved,
> but deserved:
> ** Billy Hamlyn becomes the host of a successful talk-show.
> ** Billy Hamlyn becomes a priest, rabbi or pastor.

** Bill Hamlyn becomes a psychologist
(NEED for all above: I have to give to others what I failed to receive).
** Bill Hamlyn, the athlete wins an Olympic Gold Medal.
(NEED: I have to show I'm better than others.)
** Bill Hamlyn, the "good uncle" is a child molester.
(NEED: I have to punish others to make up for the neglect I suffered)

* Billy, the teenager was considered "dumb", again and again he failed Math.
** William Hamlyn, the novelist, becomes a best selling author
(NEED: I have to prove I made may way though I was considered stupid).
** William Hamlyn, the college instructor, enjoys handing out "poor grades"
(NEED: I have to hurt others as I was hurt.)

And here are a few more suggestions;

* Show the viewer what kind of character he/she sees on the screen, by having character react specifically to other characters, events and/or situations.
* Never neglect emotional diversification. Specify characters emotional condition at every stage of your screenplay.
* Don't try to characterize via dialog only but consider physical actions.
* Create a basic emotional and mental attitude for every one of your main characters. Don't hesitate to adjust emotional reactions somewhat to your screenplay's ever changing situations.
* Have the viewer be aware of the moment when a character is about to commit himself/herself either to an issue or to another character.
* Have the viewer realize that at times unsolved issues from the past effect present issues.
* Emotional layering is important. A character should respond to other characters and/or events appropriately and within his/her established behavioral frame.
* Characters should be dynamic, strong, but never melodramatic.
* Strong, but opposing emotional desires will pull a character into different directions.
* Always look at your characters cinematically. Ask yourself," How can I show who this character is, and what as a result, this character does."
* You have heard it over and over, and here you will hear it again, contrast your characters via professions, occupations, and most importantly surrounding mood and atmosphere (setting). Two gangsters discussing a "heist" while using identical dialog, will come across differently if they meet in the Paris opera during a performance of "Figaro", at a Dodger's game, or in a border town "dive".
* If a character faces a dangerous situation, combine the characters fear with additional, possibly contradictory, emotions.

* The most interesting characters struggles show conscious GOAL either opposed or strengthened by subconscious NEED
* Actions might be mental and/or physical
    ** A character has a NEED, "I've got to get some cash," Ralph decides. "I've got to impress Liza."
    ** NEED leads to DECISION. "I'll rob a bank."
    ** Decision lead to ACTION. Ralph, wearing a wig and a false mustache enters the bank.

EFFECTIVE DIALOG MADE EASY

Script Structure keeps viewers attuned to the story, but it is dialog that makes the characters on screen come alive. On screen dialog is different from novel or stage play dialog. In a novel the reader creates his/her own vision as a character's thoughts, gestures and emotions as well as dialog are "spelled out." The drama uses dialog to verbally express intentions, thoughts and emotions. The film is different. Because of the brevity of dialog the motion picture, especially the SUSPENSE film, depends on these dialog patterns:

* Hot Narration
* Cool Narration
* Everyday Dialog
* Shifting Dominance
* Motive and Reaction Pattern

Hot Narration Hot Narration delves deeply into a character's soul. Hot narration scenes are highly emotionally charged, and -if used in moderation - will grip the viewer. If used indiscriminately, Hot Narration makes a film top heavy with emotion.

Cool Narration. Cool narration does neither hide or reveal anything. "What you hear is what you get," the viewer will receive information. Use setting, background and/or physical activities to give visual interest to a Cool Narration information segment.

EVERYDAY DIALOG The often heard advice, "listen to how people talk before you create dialog," should be taken with the proverbial "grain of salt". True, an effective movie shows the viewer a "picture of life", and dialog presents "a slice of life". Still, a film is not as much the PRESENTATION of life, as it is a REPRESENTATION of life. This means: motion picture dialog, bound to certain limitations, must define a character as a specific person.

Create real people. A character's way of speaking defines him/her as a specific person. Define each character you create by way of:

* Diction (but stay away from dialects)
* Choice of words
* Reaction to opposing dialog, characters or events
* Attitude

DIALOG REVEALS RELATIONSHIPS. Superficial dialog is boring. On screen effective dialog reveals relationships.

> BOSS
> We'll have to get the report out by five o'clock

> SECRETARY
> Yes, Mr. Smith.

No specific relationship is indicated. Now take a look at the next examples:

> BOSS
> We'll have to get the report out by five o'clock.

> SECRETARY
> Of course Mr. Smith. No problem.

The ambitious secretary wants to hold on to her job.

> BOSS
> We'll have to get the report out by five o'clock.

> SECRETARY
> By five? Can't it wait until tomorrow? I'll have to get these
> bills out first.

We look at a comfortable, trusting relationship.

> BOSS
> We'll have to get the report out by five o'clock.

> SECRETARY
> Another report? Forget about it. I have to leave early, got to
> get my nails done.

There definitely exists a "relationship". Something's going on.

<u>BANTERING.</u> Bantering adds spice to the most mundane dialog. Take a look at the following exchange:

> AMY
> You had lunch?

> BETSY
> Of course. I had a hamburger.

Boring? Right. But add a dash of BANTERING and enjoy the difference.

> AMY
> You had lunch? A hamburger?

> BETSY
> Of course I had a hamburger. What did you expect? A full
> course dinner at the Ritz?

DOMINANCE PATTERN. Shifting Dominance implies that one character is more powerful than the opposing character. You may consider this particular element of dialog construction if you are saddled with the job of giving the viewer important, but boring information. The following scene (Kevin and Anne meet in the hospital, Act II FROZEN SCREAM) shows shifting dominance levels, as well as the scene's APEX. Most scenes constructed upon the element of SHIFTING DOMINANCE feature an APEX, the moment of equality between characters. APEX adds substance and suspense.

KEVIN dominates

> KEVIN
> I had a talk with some of Bob Richard's friends. They told
> me he attended one of Dr. Gerard's - your husband's -
> seminars.

> ANNE
> So?

> KEVIN (shows photo)
> That's Bob, the missing student. Do you recognize him?

> ANNE
> Yes, I guess. I work for the college. Bob came to my office a
> few times. What about it?

> KEVIN
> I was told Bob kept kinda silent about a seminar your
> husband taught, that ...how do you call it ... longevity
> seminar. Let me ask you, did any - what shall I say -
> experimental situations take place?

Apex
> ANNE
> What kind of experiments?

> KEVIN
> I don't know. But these experiments may be the reason why
> Bob disappeared - well, vanished.

> ANNE
> Nonsense. Yes, my husband did a number of psychological
> experiments with his students - but -

Kevin dominates

                              KEVIN
          And I bet, something mighty strange must have gone on
          during these experiments.

<u>ANNE dominates</u>

                              ANNE
          Nothing strange went on, believe you me. My husband
          concentrated on altered states of consciousness. That's all.

                              KEVIN
          Kindly don't confuse me with your long-winded psychological
          terms,

                              ANNE
          And you - kindly - forget about your pulp fiction notion that
          my husband's experiments had any sinister overtones.

          It is easy to establish a dominance pattern. Here are a few suggestions:

               * Character A dominates throughout scene
               * Shifting dominance between characters A and B
               * Shifting dominance between characters A and B, while character C
                  tries to intermediate
               * Character A has dominance at the beginning of the scene, character
                  B gains dominance at end of the scene

<u>MOTIVE AND REACTION PATTERN.</u> Gives the viewer insight into either:

               * Situation and character's goal
               * Characters general and/or momentary emotional state
               * Every motive requires a reaction:
                  ** The reaction is in line with the motive
                  ** The reaction is NOT in line with the given motive
                  ** There is NO reaction to a given motive

          Let's take a look at the following example. Situation: Marlee, Eric feels, is budding
in on his project.

<u>Reaction in line with motive:</u> (Marlee hits back)

                              ERIC
          There's something we've got to talk over.

                              MARLEE
          Yes. I'm glad you've brought it up. Meyers told me about that
          remark you made about me. Called me a broad -

> ERIC
> Meyers is a darned liar. I never called you a broad. But he is right. You should have kept your mouth shut at the meeting.

> MARLEE
> Really? Let me ask you, who did all the work on the project. You or me?

Reaction not in line with motive (Marlee avoids)

> ERIC
> There's something we've got to talk over.

> MARLEE
> Later. After I finished this report.

> ERIC
> Let's talk about the meeting this morning. I'm heading the project. Right? But you did all the talking. Made yourself important. Why?

> MARLEE
> Someone had to say something. Forget about it.

No reaction to given motive (Marlee refuses to face the issue)

> ERIC
> There's something we've got to talk over.

> MARLEE
> I better get going, got an appointment...

Marlee, without looking at Eric, picks up her purse and leaves.

MAKE YOUR DIALOG REALISTIC. It is difficult for actors to "breath life" into stilted dialog or generic dialog that doesn't say much. Here is an example:

"We went to San Francisco, and from there proceeded to the Oregon border." Few people talk like that. Agreed? Most likely they'd say:

> We went to San Francisco - along the Pacific Coast Highway - less traffic - and then on to Oregon.

Diversify dialog to "fit" the characters. But go easy:

> Teenager: Went to Frisco. Bad (or neat, whatever is currently in vogue) - I'm telling you - bad

Husband: Yeah, took the family - and the dog - up to that darn
place.

Socialite: San Francisco? Lovely, simply lovely.

Newly weds: San Francisco...I guess we were there...weren't we?

People, (at least the ones I know) usually don't speak in neatly constructed sentences, they:

* Don't complete a sentence
* Interrupt others
* Interrupt themselves
* Mimic the speaker
* Disregards what has been said
* Switch to an entirely different topic

ALEX

Tomorrow we'll sail (incomplete sentence)

MARY

Right. Tomorrow we'll sail...(mimics) Got the tickets -

ALEX

- and the passports (interrupts) By the way there was
something I got to say... right... my sea sick pills, where are
they?

MARY

I saw Ruby the other day, and she said... (switches to different
topic)

RHYTHM. RHYTHM deals with intensity levels. The effective script features the intensity
levels we use (without being aware of it) in everyday speech:

* I want to explain (intensity level I)
* I want to make a point (intensity level II)
* I want to force (intensity level III)

A father discourages his son from moving to Hollywood to "pursue an acting career".

DAD

Right now is not the time to go to Hollywood. Yes, you acted
in High School plays. But an actor you ain't. That takes
training - and some maturity, if you know what I mean. (I
want to explain) How do you want to make a living in that
darn place? Parking cars? Waiting on tables? You ain't old
enough to get a job. Mother and I can't help you out. (I want
to make a point) Nothing doing. You stay here, right here.

Finish High School, go to college, prepare yourself for a decent job - and then, maybe...But now, I don't want to hear another word about you going to be a Hollywood Star. Understand? And you better listen to me (I want to force)

PACE. PACE refers to a character's mental and emotional condition at a specific MOMENT IN TIME, the scene on hand, and deals with:

* A character's relationship to other characters, environment, situations and objects.
* A character's personal PACE. Is he/she a thinker or doer, an extrovert or introvert.
* Where a character has been before the scene on hand commences, and where a character is supposed to go after the scene has been completed.
* The scene's and/or character's urgency level (emotional, physical, psychological).
* The scenes or character's lassitude (emotional, physical, psychological)

*

ENVIRONMENT MADE EASY
Environment is your SUSPENSE film's unifying element. Clearly establish the type of SUSPENSE film the viewer expects to see, via the MOOD the environment exudes. Give your viewer again and again the "feel" of a specific place during a specific moment in time. The filmmaker must be fully aware of the EMOTIONAL impact he/she needs to create. This emotional impact, however, does not deal as much with the on screen character's emotion as with the emotions the viewer experiences. Take a look at two examples:

The first example does not intent to arouse any emotion.

INTERIOR POLICE HEADQUARTERS. NIGHT. A busy place. Police officers, plain cloth detectives and a handcuffed convict. Detective ROBERTS, nodding to one of the police officers, enters his office.

INTERIOR ROBERT'S OFFICE. NIGHT.
ROBERTS walks to his desk, he reaches for a file.

The second example makes the viewer uneasy

INTERIOR POLICE HEADQUARTERS. NIGHT.
A busy place. Detective ROBERTS elbows his way through an ever shifting, noisy crowd.

ROBERTS POV. A hand cuffed prisoners looms over him.

Back on ROBERTS. For a moment he stares at the prisoner. ZOOM in on handcuffs.

Back on ROBERTS. He hurries along. Enters his office.

<u>INTERIOR ROBERTS OFFICE. NIGHT</u>
ROBERTS enters a dark cavern. The telephone rings. The babble of voices invades the office. Breathing heavily, ROBERTS leans against the door.

The way the filmmaker uses environment/mood often depends upon a particular scene's point of view.

<u>POINT OF VIEW,</u> based upon a character's momentary emotional and/or mental condition, shows the character's response to the environment shown on screen. The identical environment may be seen from various characters POINTS OF VIEW. The prisoner in his/her cell absorbs environment differently from the guard's POINT OF VIEW.

The prisoner may view his/her cell either as a cage or the haven keeping him/her safe from other prisoners. The guard my be indifferent to the prison atmosphere, he/she may be afraid or eager to exert authority. The following demonstrates the IDENTICAL ENVIRONMENT SEEN FROM THREE DIFFERENT POINTS OF VIEW and expressed via PHYSICAL ACTIONS.

<u>INTERIOR PRISON CELL. DAY</u> (Cell seen as a cage) Solitary. ZACK a caged animal stomps up and down - a few feet this way, a few feet that way. Tired of facing nothing but walls, he quickly turns to the bars. Grabs them. Presses his face against them.

Zack's POV. Bars, bars, nothing but a never ending world of iron bars.

<u>INTERIOR PRISON CELL</u> (Cell seen as safe haven) ZACK his arms covering his head, crouches in a corner. Hearing the guard approaching he curls himself into an even tighter ball.

<u>INTERIOR PRISON HALLWAY.</u> (Hallway seen as a place of authority) Guard BROWN walks along. His footsteps echo on the cement floor.

Brown's POV. The never ending row of iron bars. Iron bars right iron bars left. Faces looking at him. Hands gripping the bars.

Back on BROWN. He rises his chin and squares his shoulders. His eyes straight ahead, he keeps on marching.

At times it is provocative to establish an off-key background. Other times the film-maker should make it clear that the crime under investigation could only have been committed in a particular environment (tie-in).

* Off-Key milieu. Alphonse Taglioni, the celebrated Italian tenor was found murdered in the freezer of a fast food restaurant.
* Tie-In milieu. Alphonse Taglioni the celebrated Italian tenor was found murdered in his dressing room.

At times setting/milieu foreshadows story development:

* Wedding Day. Marie, a young heiress and Edwin a struggling law student had been married but a few hours ago. Now Edwin carries his bride across the threshold of their "honeymoon suite" - a budget motel's bedroom. Edwin struggles to turn on the light. Marie's POV. She glimpses narrow twin beds before the light flickers and dies down
* Wedding Day. Marie and Edwin two college students have eloped to be married. Now Edwin carries his bride across the threshold of their "honeymoon suite", a simple but friendly motel room. Giggling they drop down on the double bed

An unexpected event forces a character to look at environment in a different light:

INTERIOR. MADGE'S BRIGHT SUNNY KITCHEN. DAY
MADGE humming to herself, decorates BUDDY'S birthday cake. The telephone rings. Licking her fingers MADGE picks up the receiver.

> MADGE
> Hi, Buddy....guess what...

> BUDDY
> Can't talk long...I'm at the police station... got arrested...

> MADGE
> What?

> BUDDY
> Yeah...

MADGE drops the receiver, she collapses on a chair. Unable to think or feel, she stares at her hands. After a moment she leaps up, grabs the birthday cake and throws it against the window.

CU of cake and icing dripping from the curtains as rain begins to splatter.

Back on MADGE, staring helplessly. The room has turned to gray shadows. Rain now beats against the window panes.

At times environment becomes a symbol for your scripts PREMISE. Dark undercurrents fester under efficiency and order.

INTERIOR HOSPITAL EMERGENCY ROOM. NIGHT
The busiest hour of the night. Orderlies pushing gurneys, police officers bring in shot gun victims. A mother holds a sick child. Nurses, Interns - everyone is in a frantic rush. Phones shrill, voices blare over the intercom. TODD an intern huddles at a public phone. Furtively he looks around, whispers -

TODD
I'll get it for you. Don't push me -
- and hangs up.

Environment, as demonstrated in this segment's examples not only supplies background, mood and atmosphere, but is essential to plot development and characterization.

*

PART III

SELLING YOUR SUSPENSE FILM

Strange as it may sound, but before you may even consider creating a SUSPENSE FILM, you must think about SELLING it. Don't waste your time working on a project that has little chance to sell. Don't rehash a recent box office hit, but explore a topic that:

* Throws a new light on a previously successful idea.
* Turns a proven concept 180 degrees around
* Looks at events in a different way
* Explores an unusual topic

If you relay on a topical issue, make certain your film's topic will be topical at least two years from now. It takes about two years to get a film financed and produced.

Always aim for HIGH CONCEPT, but never equate HIGH CONCEPT with high budget. HIGH CONCEPT simply means a film can be advertised effectively because of it's audience grabbing HOOK.

Next familiarize yourself with the questions a distribution company may ask:

* Does the film have marketing potentials
* Is the setting interesting
* Are the characters well drawn
* Is this SUSPENSE film sellable without a star name attached to it
* Is the story too predictable
* Does the plot feature suspense, twists and conflicts
* Are interpersonal relationships interesting

Now a word of warning: as unique your film's plot might be, as grabbing it's HOOK, as tantalizing the topic, as exiting plot and characters are, your SUSPENSE film might not find distribution if it is above the average viewer's understanding. Always, therefore, keep the AVERAGE VIEWER in mind.

You will find the names, addresses and telephone numbers of distribution companies in these publications:

* Pacific Coast Studio Directory
* Hollywood Blue Book
* Hollywood Creative Directory

Samuel French book stores, Los Angeles and New York, carry the above listed directories. But be careful, before you hand over your film to just any distribution company find out:

* How long has the distributor been in business, titles of films they have released recently, and do they distribute films that are budget wise similar to yours.

* What is the distributor's area of concentration: Domestic theatrical and home video, Foreign distribution all areas, Cable
* How do they plan to market your film. Will your film be shows at the major motion picture sales exhibits, Cannes Film Festival France - MIFED (Milan) Italy and AFMA Los Angeles.
* Will your film be distributed in the off-season (April-June, August - November). A low budget film has a much better change to succeed in the off- season
* How many prints will be cut
* Advertising (ask for tear off sheets).
* Will exhibitors share advertising cost. At times advertising costs are shared: Producer pays 50% distributor and exhibitor pay 25% each.
* Ask for the distribution schedule
* Find out about percentage of box office receipts:
    ** 20% off floor to exhibitor
    ** Producer and distributor share the remaining 80% fifty-fifty

Find out whether or not your distributor handles auxiliary rights such as Cable and home video. There must be a negotiated time period between your film's theatrical and cable exposure. Cable, most likely will either give the producer an advance, or via negative pickup will buy your film outright. Usually the filmmaker receives payments in four equal installments stretched out over a year. As far as home video tape sales are concerned the distributor will retain 60% of a tape's retail price. Low Budget Independent home video films are sold for $39.95 a tape. The producer has to supply duplication and box covers, (sleeves).

Foreign sales are complicated. Often the US distributor works together with a foreign distributor. The distributors share between 35-40% distribution fees. The foreign buyer sends a letter of credit (LC) to the foreign distributor who in turns submits the LC to the US distributor. Sometimes it takes months to cash in the LC, and since there is always the danger the LC will be canceled DO NOT release your film until the LC has been cashed. You are expected to submit the following:

* Negative copy of your film, optical sound track, Dialog track, music track, sound effect track
* Titles, textless background for title
* Cover shots for TV
* Digital TV master
* Black and white stills, color slides
* Advertising (art work one sheets)
* Script (English version)

In case distributors fail to react favorably to your SUSPENSE film, don't give up, but go the film festival route. Most festivals accept full length feature films. For more information write to:

* Association of Independent
Video and Filmmakers (AIVF)
625 Broadway
New York, NY 10012

During the past ten years the Majors forced many hard working Independents out of business. Today, films produced by majors and mini-majors dominate the domestic theater screen as well as the home video market. Major films hit the home video market a few months or even weeks after one has seen these multimillion dollar films on the domestic theatrical screen. But lately it seems, the Independents are coming back. Most likely you won't find their star-less, low budget films on American theater screen, but you will find their films on the shelves of video stores.

Since VCR's are now more affordable in East European countries as well as South America and Africa, the Independent's main business (at the time of this writing) is overseas video and theatrical distribution. These distribution areas demand simple, <u>family type stories</u> long on visuals and shot on dialog. Dubbing, after all, is expensive.

Presently the domestic theatrical home video business seems to undergo a dramatic change. My prediction is (hopefully I am right) that, though some home video distributors still demand their product to be shot on 35mm (an expensive process) changes are approaching fast. Digital process, otoscope effects, digitally created virtual sets (terrific for special effects) are revolutionizing the home video field. A tape or digitally produced home video film, not only is much less expensive to shoot, but more economical to produce. Since Major Studios burdened with high overheads are not interested in the "low budget, exclusively made for home video product" I predict the Independents will surge ahead. Only, never confuse Low Budget with mediocre artistic quality. The term Low Budget refers to a film less costly to produce because of:

* Fewer locations
* Less characters
* No expensive special effects and/or action scenes.

If the filmmaker requires special effects and/or action scenes, he/she should choose "generic effects" stock shots from existing films. A number of motion pictures supply specialty stores sell stock shots fairly inexpensively.

Possibly you are not as much interested in producing a SUSPENSE film, but you are ready to sell your terrific SUSPENSE film script. So, let's discuss:

* Where can I sell my screenplay
   ** Major studios and mini-majors including Network TV and cable
   ** Independent production companies
* Do I need an agent, and how do I get an agent

<u>MAJOR STUDIOS AND MINI-MAJORS</u> Forget about submitting your script to any major studio or mini-major, network TV or cable. Your unsolicited script will be returned unopened. These companies work with well established agents only.

<u>INDEPENDENTS.</u> You will find the addresses of Independent companies in the previously listed directories. Call, find out whether or not the Independent is interested in the kind of script you plan to submit and get the name of a contact person. Never try to sell your screenplay's idea over the phone. If necessary ask for an appointment to "pitch" your idea. Never submit your script "cold" but:

* Register your script with WGA (Writers Guild of America). You do not have to be a member.

Writers Guild of America - West
7000 West Third Street
Los Angeles, CA 90048-4329
Writers Guild of America - East
555 West 57th Street
New York, NY 10019

* Include a release form:
    ** Your name, title of screenplay
    ** Certification that you:
        *** are screenplay's sole owner
        *** you own all rights to the screenplay
    ** If the screenplay is based on actual events and/or living or dead persons, add copy of release, agreement and (if applicable) copy of "Errors and Omissions" policy.
* State that you are aware that production company may have access to material similar to yours. You will not request compensation in the event if any plot similar to yours might appear on the company's production schedule. (Highly unfair, I agree, but a recognized part of any submission.)
* Mention that you have retained a copy of the screenplay
* Add information why you are qualified to deal with the screenplay's topic (attorney, police officer, teacher, doctor).
* Write REQUESTED MATERIAL on the envelope

A small Independent, most likely, won't buy your script outright. Since you do not know how affluent this company is and whether or not your script ultimately will be produced, do not give them the script on speculation, but insist on an option payment. Give an option for six months only, after that, for another payment, the option may be renewed. Once a production company purchases your screenplay, make certain the contract contains the following:

* A definite purchase price
* A definite payment schedule
    ** Partial payment to begin at the beginning of pre-production
    ** Partial payment at commencement of principal photography
* Screen writer's credit to appear on front titles

<u>DO I NEED AN AGENT AND HOW DO I GET AN AGENT</u> Having a knowledgeable agent "in your corner" can make your career. But stay away from agents advertising for "new and talented writers." These individuals are not in the business of selling your script, they make a few - somewhat legitimate dollars - by advising you about your script and/or rewriting your script. Since Hollywood is still the center of film activities, you will do much better choosing a Los Angeles based agency. If a New York agency is interests in representing you, make certain they have a Los Angeles affiliation. Consider a WGA (Writers's Guild of America) franchised agent ONLY. You do not have to be a WGA member to request their agent list.

It is best to sign with an established agency. New agents (though WGA franchised) have difficulties to open the proverbial "doors". Still, a new agency is better than no agent. Once an agent is interested in representing you, don't fail to find out:

* How many writers does the agent present
  How many screenplays did the agency sell during the previous year
    (this includes options and actual sales)
* Names of buyers (production companies)

*

PART IV

FROZEN SCREAM

A Horror Film

(Act I)
EXTERIOR ROAD. NIGHT.
A fog shrouded, rain splashed country road. Headlights cutting through the fog and driving rain come closer and closer until they fill the screen.

INTERIOR ANNE'S CAR.
Wipers screech. ANNE, gripping the steering wheel, gazes through the curtain of rain slashing against the windshield. She picks up her car phone, dials.

> ANNE
> Tom...Tom...come on...

SUPERIMPOSE: BEACH. NIGHT. A group of young people TOM and FATHER O'BRIAN amongst them, chanting surround a flaming Solstice log. Anne steps away from them, looks around

Back on ANNE, on the phone.

> ANNE
> Tom...please...

SUPERIMPOSE: BEACH. NIGHT.
On Father O'Brian and TOM. TOM breaks away, yells

> TOM
> Here I come, brave new world...

ANNE steps up to Father O'Brian.

> ANNE
> What happened?

> FATHER O'BRIAN
> Tom wanted me to hear his confession. I had to refuse absolution.

FADE OUT.

INTERIOR ANNE's CAR. Back on ANNE

> ANNE
>
> Are you all right?

TOM's voice comes over the speaker phone.

> TOM (V.O)
> No... Call Father O'Brian... he's got to hear my
> confession...grant absolution...

A distorted voice breaks through

> VOICE (V.O.)
> The angels are here Tom.

> TOM (V.O.)
> No...no...no... Father....O'...Brian

> ANNE
> Tom...

> VOICE (V.O.)
> Get ready for the angels

> ANNE
> Tom...

ANNE hangs up. Shaking with fear she dials

> ANSWERING MACHINE (V.O.)
> Father O'Brian speaking. Greetings my friends, this is a
> mechanical salutation.

ANNE bangs the receiver down

EXTERIOR VICTORIAN MANSION. NIGHT.
A square Victorian building. Rain pours down. Thunder rolls, lightening flashes. ANNE'S car
drives up. ANNE exits her car and runs across the yard. She throws the front door open and
rushes into the house.

INTERIOR VICTORIAN MANSION. HALLWAY. NIGHT
ANNE enters. She turns on the light switch but the hallway remains dark. Her voice almost
drowned by thunder, ANNE yells-

> ANNE
> Tom.

There is no answer. ANNE fumbles for the light switch. The hallway remains dark, Fumbling
through her purse, ANNE pulls out a flashlight, a dim stream of light wavering, she rushes to
the staircase, makes her way through the hallway to the stairs.

The grandfathers's clock on the landing strikes two o'clock. Taken aback, ANNE stops for a moment before she hurries up the stairs.

INTERIOR VICTORIAN MANSION. STAIRCASE. NIGHT
ANNE hurries up the staircase. Her flashlight wavers, lightening flashes, thunder rolls.

INTERIOR VICTORIAN MANSION. UPPER HALLWAY. NIGHT
Thunder echoes through the hallway. ANNE, almost falling, stumbles to a door. Throws the door open.

INTERIOR VICTORIAN MANSION. STUDY. NIGHT.
A flash of light across a paper littered desk. Then - darkness.

On ANNE huddling against the door.

ANNE's POV, her flashlight wavers across some upturned chairs, books littering the floor.

Back on ANNE. She turns.

INTERIOR VICTORIAN MANSION. UPPER HALLWAY. NIGHT
ANNE stops at a partially open door. Enters.

INTERIOR VICTORIAN MANSION. BEDROOM. NIGHT.
By now thunder threatens from far away, lightening has grown weaker, but rain still pounds. ANNE walks through the room. The flashlight's beam traces over a double bed. ANNE calls out softly -

                              ANNE
                    Tom....
ANNE's POV.

SHOCK ZOOM. Tom sprawls in the corner. His shirt is open, blood covers his chest, electrodes protrude from his forehead. His eyes stare.

Back on ANNE. A silent scream.

                         VOICE (V.O)
                    The angels are here.

Hands - almost a caress - slide up ANNE's arms to her shoulders and from there to her throat.

Frozen, slowly - ever so slowly - ANNE turns her head.

ANNE's POV. Barely visible against the dark hallway, as black hooded figure looms behind her.

(NOTE: Act I introduces protagonist and establishes environment. Main Question: Why was Tom killed?)

ACT II

<u>INTERIOR HOSPITAL. ANNE'S ROOM. DAY.</u>
ANNE tossing and turning.

ANNE
The angels...the angels...killed Tom

Faces rush up to her. First a NURSE with a syringe - then SVEN, his voice comes from far away.

SVEN
Calm down, everything will be all right.

SVEN's face disintegrates. Now LIL's face rushes up to ANNE

LIL
No one killed Tom

ANNE (hardly audible)
The angels...

LIL
Tom died of a heart attack

LIL's face and voice fade out.

<u>ESTABLISHING SHOT HOSPITAL DAY.</u>

<u>INTERIOR HOSPITAL. ANNE'S ROOM. DAY.</u>

LIL stands next to ANNE'S bed. By now, ANNE has calmed down.

LIL
Believe me, Tom succumbed to a heart attack.

ANNE
But the electrodes, I'm telling you -

LIL
Let's face it, you've been under a lot of pressure during the past two years. Tom -

ANNE
Yes Tom was -

LIL
- was not easy to live with. We all know that. And there's clinical proof that stress can cause hallucinations.

                              ANNE
                You mean to tell me the electrodes -

                               LIL
                - and those darn angel voices -

                              ANNE
                - and the black hooded figure -

                               LIL
                - especially that Frankenstein - were nothing but tricks your
                mind played on you, my pet.

LIL sits down on the bed. She takes ANNE's hands into hers.

                               LIL
                There's something else. Tom's parents insisted upon crema-
                tion. They took the ashes back to New York.

For a long time ANNE looks at LIL

                              ANNE
                I won't ever see him again...Tom

The telephone rings. LIL picks up, she listens for a moment than nods

                               LIL
                A detective McGuire wants to have a chat with you. About
                fourteen days ago one of Tom's student disappeared. Are you
                up to see the guy?

                              ANNE
                Sure, why not.

LIL hangs up. She rises. Then a crisp wave of her hand.

                               LIL
                Gotta run. See you later.

LIL leaves.

                            LIL (VO)
                Go right in Detective, but make it short and snappy.

There is a knock on the door.

                              ANNE
                Come on in.

The door opens and DETECTIVE KEVIN McGUIRE enters.

INTERIOR HOSPITAL. HALLWAY. DAY.
Nurses, orderlies, patients. On LIL walking along. SVEN catches up with her.

                    SVEN
          How is Anne?

                    LIL
          What do you expect? Anyway -

INTERIOR HOSPITAL, ANNE'S ROOM. DAY.

                    KEVIN
          I had a talk with some of Bob Richard's friends. They told me
          he attended one of Dr. Gerard's - your husband's -seminars.

                    ANNE
          So? What about?

KEVIN pulls a photo from his attache case. He hands it to ANNE CU on BOB's photo

                    KEVIN (V.O.)
          That's Bob the missing student. Do you -

Back on KEVIN and ANNE

                    KEVIN
          - recognize him?
ANNE hands the photo back.

                    ANNE
          Yes, I guess. I work for the college. I'm Dr. Johnson's
          secretary. Bob came to my office a few times. What about it?

There is a uncomfortable pause.
                    KEVIN
          I was told Bob kept somewhat silent about the seminar your
          husband taught...that ...how do you call it...longevity
          seminar.

A Nurse enters, during the next few lines she checks Anne's pulse, gathers up an empty glass,
and leaves.

                    KEVIN
          Let me ask you, did any - what shall I say - experimental
          situations take place?

                              ANNE
          Situations? What kind of -

                             KEVIN
          I don't know. But these experiments may be the reason why
          Bob disappeared - well, vanished.

                              ANNE
          Nonsense. True, my husband did a number of psychological
          experiments with his students, but -

                             KEVIN
          And I bet, something mighty strange must have gone on
          during these experiments.

                              ANNE
          Nothing strange went on, believe you me. My husband
          concentrated on altered states of consciousness. That's all.

KEVIN holds ANNE's gaze.

                             KEVIN
          Kindly don't confuse me with your longwinded psychological
          terms, but -

                              ANNE
          And you - kindly -forget about your pulp fiction notion that
          my husband's experiments had any sinister overtones

(NOTE: Lil, Antagonist, established. Kevin, Protagonist Sub- Plot established. Question 1:
What happened to Bob. Question 2: Do criminal experiments take place at South Coast
College. Forward movement Main Plot: Tom's possible criminal activities. Forward movement
Sub-Plot: Anne meets Kevin.)

EXTERIOR BEACH. DAY.
A sunny, bright day. On waves rushing and crashing against the beach. On ANNE and LIL
walking along.

                              ANNE
          - and that conceited excuse of a police detective suggested
          there was something - quote - "mighty strange" going on in
          Tom's seminars.

ANNE looks up. Her POV seagulls streaking across the sky.

                            LIL (VO)
          What did you tell him?

Back on ANNE and LIL

                              ANNE
          What could I've told him? I babbled something about altered
          states of consciousness.

Silently they walk along the beach. Surf pounds.

                              LIL
          Miss Tom?

                              ANNE
          Very much

                              LIL
          Mhm

                              ANNE
          You know my marriage was not - what shall I say - happy.
          Ever since he took over that darned longevity research -

                              LIL
          - he moved...emotionally...away from you. Well, what can I
          tell you... Tom was a dedicated scientist.

                              ANNE
          Like Sven

                              LIL
          Right. Like Sven.

Silently they walk along.

                              ANNE
          Thanks for letting me spend the weekend with you. I hope I
          didn't butt in between Sven and you.

                              LIL
          Heavens, no. Sven is a happy as a clam puttering around in
          that stupid lab of his. Don't be silly. I don't owe him
          anything.
                              ANNE
          I often wondered - hope, you don't mind me asking it - what
          do you see in Sven? He is so much older than you are.
          And...he's such a pompous ass.

                              LIL
          I don't know. Sven is a cold blooded bastard, but...I guess...he
          appeals to my... craving for danger and adventure.

Laughing, LIL runs off. ANNE picks up a handful of sand, throws the sand at LIL

                                    ANNE
          I bet.

(Note: Forward movement Main Plot: Sven owns a private lab. There is a connection between LIL and SVEN. ANNE and LIL are friends.)

EXTERIOR BEACH. DAY
On Surfers. KEVIN, carrying his surfboard, walks along. KEVIN goes to his van, opens it, and secures the surfboard.

EXTERIOR LIL's HOUSE. DAY
LIL carrying a makeup case and ANNE carrying an overnighter walk up to ANNE's car.

                                    LIL
          I wish you' wouldn't go back to your Victorian monster. That
          house gives me the creeps.

ANNE opens the trunk, deposits her overnighter. She takes the makeup case from LIL.

                                    LIL
          Why don't you rent a smart little apartment in town?

                                    ANNE
          It was my parents house. I grew up there. Couldn't live
          anywhere else.

ANNE closes the trunk, she opens the car door.

                                    LIL
          Hell, why not? That place breeds bad dreams like mosquitos.

                                    ANNE
          Thanks for a lovely weekend.

                                    LIL
          Have a safe trip. See you Monday in the office. Don't be late.
          Sven will be glad to have you back.

ANNE gets into the car, she buckles up, starts the engine, waves to LIL, and drives off.

On LIL, waving. A strange smile flashes over her face.

EXTERIOR FAST FOOD RESTAURANT. DUSK.
The restaurants flashing neon sign sends streaks of light into the darkening sky. ANNE's car drives up. She gets out and enters the restaurant.

<u>INTERIOR FAST FOOD RESTAURANT. NIGHT.</u>
A line of suntanned backs, cut off jeans. ANNE, waiting patiently takes some dollar bills from her purse.

> KEVIN (V.O)
> Fish sandwich - - French Fries - a coffee, regular - -

ANNE, notices KEVIN.

> KEVIN
> - - no cream.

ANNE steps up to the counter.

> ANNE
> Make mine a fish sandwich too.

KEVIN turns, looks at ANNE. ANNE smiles.

> ANNE
> Tom never liked fish, reminded him too much the way he grew up Catholic. I haven't had seafood for years.

> KEVIN
> I know. Fish on Friday, go to hell for a hot dog. I grew up Catholic too.

Both pay for their food, take their trays. KEVIN points to a booth.

> KEVIN
> Mind to join me?

> ANNE
> Yes, why not.

On ANNE and KEVIN walking up to a booth. They put their trays on the table and sit down. Ever so often someone walks by.

> KEVIN
> I was kind of worried when I left the hospital. Well..I was a bit aggressive.

ANNE nods. She sprinkles some ketchup over her French Fries.

> KEVIN
> Matter of fact I wanted to come back -

> ANNE
> Honest?

                    KEVIN
...just to say "hello" and bring some flowers to cheer you up.

                    ANNE
Flowers? Really? That's kind of you, detective.

                    KEVIN
Kevin, if you don't's mind. But that dragon of a head nurse,
wouldn't let me see you.

ANNE laughs a little. She bites into her sandwich. KEVIN takes a sip of coffee.

                    KEVIN
Getting back to Dr. Gerard's dislike of fish. It seems he
resented the Church and her teachings. Didn't he?

                    ANNE
I have the distinct impression you're well informed about
everything concerning my late husband. So why ask me
about his theological likes or dislikes?

                    KEVIN
Forgive me, I shouldn't have mentioned Dr. Gerard.

                    ANNE
Well, you did. So, what do you have on your mind. Go
ahead, spit it out.

                    KEVIN
I've heard he and Father O'Brian spent much time together.

                    ANNE
They were friends as well as adversaries. They argued about
religion.

                    KEVIN
Did they argue about Dr. Gerard's research?

                    ANNE
Why do you ask?

                    KEVIN
I have a hunch - and believe me, at this point it's only a
hunch -
                    ANNE
Go on.

KEVIN

- that your husband's death and Bob's disappearance are ...in some strange way... connected.

ANNE

How?

KEVIN

I don't know. But there is something - and that's what I am after - that may tie the disappearance and your husband's death together.

A waitress comes by, refills their cups.

KEVIN

I found out that Dr. Johnson -

ANNE

Sven?

KEVIN

Yes, Sven Johnson and your husband had these...well...discussions.

ANNE

They had arguments. Yes. Nothing about it. Everyone at South Coast College knows about Sven's mental acrobatics.

KEVIN

I see.

KEVIN taps the rim of his mug. Puzzled, ANNE looks at him.

KEVIN

Did Dr. Gerard... ever receive an offer of employment from an Ivy league university?

ANNE

Not that I know of. What are you getting at.

KEVIN

Well, there is the - unlikely - possibility, that one or the other of these institutions tried to get their hands on the longevity research by offering a posh job to one of researchers.

ANNE

You mean, you suspect Tom of trying to sell out? Behind Sven's back?

                              KEVIN
          Exactly. And Bob, his student - I guess - was involved in the
          deal. Industrial espionage is not uncommon in academia. -
          Let's get out of here.

ANNE and KEVIN get up. They empty their trays. ANNE holds on to her coffee.

                              ANNE
          The longevity research...is it that important?

                              KEVIN
          It is. I guess.

EXTERIOR FAST FOOD RESTAURANT. PARKING LOT. NIGHT
ANNE and KEVIN walk up to ANNE's car.

                              ANNE
          And you mean Sven found out about Tom's -

                              KEVIN
          Sorry...deceit -

                              ANNE
          And killed him.

ANNE'S eyes tear into KEVIN

                              KEVIN
          Yes, there is reason to believe Dr. Gerard was murdered.

Warm and comforting KEVIN covers ANNE's hand with his.

                              KEVIN
          But as far as the department is concerned your husband died
          of natural causes.

                              ANNE
          And off the record?

                              KEVIN
          Off the record? There is the possibility of foul play.

                              ANNE
          Let's do something about it. Let's find Tom's killer.

                              KEVIN
          That's not easy. First I have to investigate that seminar, find
          out what went on.

There is a moment silence. KEVIN looks at ANNE.

> KEVIN
> And that takes a search warrant. But without due cause I
> cannot get a search warrant.

> ANNE
> That means you need a very good reason to search any
> premise.

KEVIN nods.

> ANNE
> All right, so why don't I try to find a bit of evidence? I work
> for Sven, I have access to files and -

> KEVIN
> Too dangerous. Don't get involved. Don't ever let Sven
> Johnson suspect anything.

(NOTE: Main Question repeated: Why was Tom killed? Question 1 repeated: What happened to Bob? Question 3: Did Sven kill Tom. Forward movement Main Plot: Sven, Kevin agrees, possibly murdered Tom. Anne decides to do some "snooping". Forward movement Sub-Plot: Anne and Kevin are attracted to each other.)

VICTORIAN MANSION. NIGHT.
Moonlight filters through the treetops. ANNE exits her car. She walks up to the house - and stops.

ANNE's POV. Clearly outlined against the backdrop of filtering moonlight and clouds a man walks up to her. Shoulders slightly stooped, head tilted he carries fishing tackle and a minnow bucket

> ANNE (freezes)
> Tom...

The moon breaking through the clouds throws a jagged pattern of light over the man's tattered jeans and plaid shirt, the clothes ANNE had seen splattered with blood.

> ANNE
> Tom...

Stiffly, every step a torture, she walks up to the man.

> MAN
> Good evening, Miss

A stranger nods to ANNE then walks off. ANNE turns and runs back to the mansion. She throws the door open and enters.

(NOTE: Surprise moment.)

<u>INTERIOR VICTORIAN MANSION. HALLWAY. NIGHT.</u>
Shadows hover in the hallway. ANNE slams the door, she leans against it, catches her breath,

CU on ANNE's hand locking the front door.

Back on ANNE She listens for a moment to the grandfather clock ticking the time away, before she moves through the hallway to the living room and enters.

<u>INTERIOR VICTORIAN MANSION. LIVING ROOM. NIGHT</u>
ANNE fumbles for the light switch. Dim light floods through the room. Taking a few steps ANNE surveys the room.

ANNE'S POV. Slow pan from the Victorian settee, the picture of a long forgotten ancestor, an old fashioned desk, cluttered with books and papers, to the 18th century mirror hanging over the fireplace.

Back on ANNE. She walks up to the mirror and brushes off some spiderwebs.

SOUND OVER: Footsteps, slowly - ever so slowly - approach the living room.

ANNE holding her breath hurriedly tiptoes to the light switch. Turns it off. Moonlight touching the walls keeps her a prisoner. And again the sound of footsteps, coming closer and closer.

ANNE grabs the poker leaning against the fireplace. Waits. The footsteps halt. Silence. And then a creaking sound. Inch by inch the door leading from the hallway to the living room opens.

Frozen, ANNE turns her head. And there it is...

ANNE'S POV. Reflected in the mirror, faintly illuminated by the bluish light seeping through the window - she sees Tom. Tom's eyes look straight at her.

Without letting her eyes waver from Tom's reflection ANNE lifts the poker.

                              CATHERINE (V.O.)
                  I hope...

On CATHERINE. Catherine a beautiful young woman, suitcase in hand, stands in the door way.

                                  CATHERINE
                ...I didn't startle you.

                            ANNE (hiding the poker)
                How did you get in?

                              CATHERINE
            The front door was unlocked.

                                ANNE
            No it was locked, I know. I locked it.

                              CATHERINE
            Didn't Lil call? She was worried. She doesn't like you all
            alone out here. She asked me to spend a few days with you.

                                ANNE
            I know you are Lil's assistant. But that means you don't have
            to keep an eye on me.

                              CATHERINE
            Course not, but -

(NOTE: Forward movement Main Plot: Establish Catherine).

INTERIOR VICTORIAN MANSION. KITCHEN. DAY
Early morning sunshine makes the old fashioned kitchen a cozy place. CATHERINE, wearing
a robe, sits at the kitchen table. She sips coffee. ANNE, a straw purse slung over her shoulder
stands next to her.

                                ANNE
            If anyone calls, I'm running a few errands. Go to the library,
            maybe drop by Father O'Brian to deliver some things for the
            church's annual jumble sale -

INTERIOR VICARAGE. OFFICE. DAY

                                ANNE
            I came...to be honest.. to ask you about Tom's last confession,
            Father.
                               O'BRIAN
            Have you forgotten that the seal of secrecy protects every
            confession?

FATHER O'BRIAN walks up to a row of plants blooming on the window sill. Turning his back
to ANNE he snips off some dead leaves.

                               O'BRIAN
            Why don't you ask me whether or not I believe Tom died of
            natural causes?

                                ANNE
            Tom was murdered, right?

                    O'BRIAN
        I don't believe so. My own hypothesis points more to suicide.

                    ANNE
        Tom would never commit a mortal sin.

FATHER O'BRIAN turns. He faces ANNE

                    O'BRIAN
        Why not? Tom had neither respect nor regard for the
        teachings of the Church.

                    ANNE
        Then why did he insist that you hear his confession?

                    O'BRIAN
        Maybe it was a last reaching out, before -

Again FATHER O'BRIAN snips off some dead leaves.

On ANNE anxiously waiting for the priest's answer

Back on FATHER O'BRIAN

                    O'BRIAN
        ... before he went into the unknown...
        ... the "brave new world."

The priest walks back to ANNE. He faces her.

                    O'BRIAN
        Tom said, "Father I am afraid to leap into the "brave new
        world" help me by hearing my confession. Could this
        ..."world"...be in any way connected to Tom's and Sven's
        research?

ANNE rises, she walks to the window, looks out.

                    O'BRIAN
        You know more about the research than I do. You were
        married to Tom.

                    ANNE
        He never told me anything.

                    O'BRIAN
        But you work for Sven Johnson. He heads the project.

ANNE

I am Sven's secretary. I have nothing to do with either the research or the seminars, and -

Eagerly the priest interrupts

O'BRIAN

But both - the research and the seminars - in some way - are connected?

ANNE

I guess so...maybe.

O'BRIAN

Mrs. McGowen, a parishioner of ours, runs a boarding house. One of her boarders, Bob Richards disappeared-

ANNE

He was one of Tom's students.

O'BRIAN

All right, there is some chance - a slight chance - that he - inadvertently - might have mentioned something...just about anything... to his landlady.

(NOTE: Question 4: What did Tom confess?)

EXTERIOR MCGOWEN'S BOARDING HOUSE. ESTABLISHING SHOT DAY

INTERIOR McGOWEN'S BOARDING HOUSE. LIVING ROOM. DAY
A red plush nightmare, where "paint by numbers" art works and bowling trophies compete for wall space. MRS. MCGOWEN, a splendidly impressive lady presides over an equally splendid silver Tea Set. A barrage of words flows from MRS. MCGOWEN'S mouth.

MRS. MCGOWEN

Missing? Possibly dead? Don't you believe it. Bob - that cheating bastard - excuse the expression - is as much alive as you and I.

ANNE

I don't get it, you mean -

MRS. MCGOWEN

Skipped. The guy skipped. Owes me a whole months rent. Yes, that's true. Not to mention the dough for water and electricity I had to cough up. And what's worse, the police won't believe me.

ANNE

What precisely is it the police won't believe you?

MRS. MCGOWEN lifts the teapot.

> MRS. MCGOWEN
> Let me warm up your tea, my dear.

> ANNE
> Just a drop or two, please.

Carefully holding a napkin under the spout, MRS. MCGOWEN fills ANNE's cup.

> MRS. MCGOWEN
> That detective - what's his name?

> ANNE
> McGuire.

> MRS. MCGOWEN
> Right, McGuire - didn't even listen when I told him I saw
> Bob.

Glowing with anticipation, ready to deliver a sermon, MRS. MCGOWEN settles back on the sofa.

> MRS. MCGOWEN
> Had done my weeks shopping at the Piggly-Wiggly. It's a bit
> far from here, right? But they give double coupons - and I
> just love their pies. Well, anyway, what was I going to say? -
> Yes, I come out, push my cart - and there he was -

> ANNE
> Are you sure it was Bob.

> MRS. MCGOWEN
> I mean, I swear on the Bible, it was Bob. "You miserable, low
> down cheat," I yell," where's my rent?" And -

Exhausted MRS. MCGOWEN drains her tea.

> ANNE
> And - what?

> MRS. MCGOWEN
> Nothing. He was gone.

> ANNE
> Did Bob ever mention anything about the classes he took at
> South Coast?

MRS. MCGOWEN shakes her head.

> ANNE
> Or any seminar he attended? A seminar my husband or Dr.
> Johnson conducted?

MRS. MCGOWEN, again, shakes her head.

> ANNE
> Any friends Bob hung around with, who - maybe attended
> the seminar?

> MRS. MCGOWEN
> McGuire already asked me... That detective is quite a hunk of
> a man, makes one's heart go BOOM, BOOM - know what I
> mean?

MRS. MCGOWEN snaps her fingers.

> MRS. MCGOWEN
> Come to think of it. There was someone. A looker. Kinda
> classy.

MRS. MCGOWEN lumbers to her desk and digs out a photo.

> MRS. MCGOWEN
> Much to ritzy for a looser like Bob.

ANNE joins her at the desk. MRS. MCGOWEN hands ANNE the photo.

> MRS. MCGOWEN
> That one tried to talk Bob into -

CU on photo. CATHERINE, blond mane flowing, her arms around BOB.

> MRS. MCGOWEN (V.O.)
> - some kinda outlandish research project.

(NOTE: Question 1 answered: Nothing happened to Bob, he is still around. Question 5: Does
Catherine recruit for any secret seminar/experiment?)

EXTERIOR VICTORIAN MANSION. DAY. The bright morning has given way to an overcast afternoon. A croquet game is in progress. Noisily, ANNE, LIL, CATHERINE and a young
student SHAWN, propel wooden balls through iron hoops, the "gates".

LIL moves her croquet ball next to ANNE's

                              LIL
           Death, like cancer is a disease we'll conquer some day.

LIL leans back, with one swift move she hits the ball through the "gate". ANNE follows LIL's move, but her ball stops short of the "gate".

                           CATHERINE
              We may say everyone of us - - will be -

She lifts her mallet, hits the ball.

CU her ball pushes ANNE's ball out of the field.

                           CATHERINE
                    - immortal.

Back on the group. CATHERINE smiles at SHAWN. It is a devastating smile.

                           CATHERINE
                Come on Shawn. Hit the ball.

Clumsily, his eyes on CATHERINE, Shawn tries to get a ball through the "gate".

                           CATHERINE
                  Come on, you can do it.

SHAWN gives it another try. CATHERINE steps closely behind him. Closing one arm around the young man, she guides his strike.

The wooden ball zooms across the lawn right into a "gate."

CATHERINE not letting go of SHAWN smiles a secret little smile

                           CATHERINE
            To be immortal, to be forever young, always in love -

SHAWN drinks in CATHERINE's smile.

                              SHAWN
              Right. That's my definition of heaven on earth.

                              LIL
                    Immortality -

An inner fire illuminates LIL'S face.

                              LIL
                 This letter stand for immortality.

She rises her hand. Against the horizon, a sky without movement or color her hand traces the Greek ATHANATOS symbol. From far away the sound of cymbals swings through the air. ANNE tenses. She puts her mallet down.

> ANNE
> I better get dinner ready.

(NOTE: Question 5 answered: Catherine recruits. Forward movement Main Plot: Catherine recruits for some secret seminars)

INTERIOR VICTORIAN MANSION. KITCHEN
Shadows hover in every corner. ANNE enters. Suddenly she stops, freezes. Then slowly, ever so slowly she turns.

ANNE's POV, a hooded shadow hovers behind the kitchen window. The shadow raises his hand and draws the ANATHATOS sign on the window. Again the sound of cymbals comes up.

INTERIOR SOUTH COAST COLLEGE. SVEN'S OUTER OFFICE.
The sound of Cymbals turns to the shrill ringing of a phone.

CU, ANNE's hand tracing the ATHANATOS sign on a sheet of college stationary. PULL Back, ANNE seated at her desk. She picks up the phone.

> ANNE
> South Coast College. Dr. Johnson's office...three o'clock...yes
> I'll notify Dr. Johnson. Thank you.

Dr. Michner, South Coast's president walks up to her.

> DR. MICHNER
> Good to have you back Mrs. Gerard. Sorry about Tom. But
> that's life, we all got to go.

ANNE hands him some mail.

> ANNE
> Here's your mail, Dr. Michner.

Dr. Michner flips through his mail

> SVEN (V.O.)
> Art - wait a minute -

SVEN walks in

> SVEN
> - about that department meeting -

Sven turns to ANNE

                    SVEN
          I've arranged for a little get together tonight - students and
          faculty -

Suzy a part time student enters with her mailcert. She collects some outgoing mail from ANNE's
desk.

                    SVEN
          Hope you can make it, Anne. Eight o'clock in my house.

                    ANNE
          Thank you. Look forward to it.

SVEN, turns to Dr. Michner, both walk to the door -

                    SVEN
          If we change the syllabus -
- and leaves.

SUZY looks at ANNE, it is obvious she has to get something off her chest. She picks up a
pencil, puts it down, tries to say something, but doesn't.

                    ANNE
          Anything wrong?

                    SUZY
          Well -

Now Suzy grabs an eraser. Throws it up in the air, catches it. ANNE waits patiently.

                    SUZY
          May I ask you something?

                    ANNE
          Sure. Go ahead.

                    SUZY
          Catherine. She rooms with you. Ain't she?

                    ANNE
          Sort of.
                    SUZY
          Is there anything going on between her and Shawn?

                        ANNE
        Catherine is in her late twenties, she's much too old for
        Shawn. I wouldn't worry if I were you.

                        SUZY
        Are you kidding? Some guys fall for older women. Last
        semester that bitch made a big play for Bob. And believe it or
        not, the jerk fell for it. Look, Shawn and I have kinda an
        agreement. We're going to get engaged...kind of.

Suzy reaches into he mail cart and throws some letters on ANNE's desk.

                        SUZY
        Now I'm going to loose him. That's for sure. Bob changed -
        that one became really a weirdo, after Catherine talked him
        into registering for that stupid longevity stuff.

                        ANNE
        What about that seminar. Please tell me.

SUZY shakes her head.

                        ANNE
        Tell me, maybe I can help you. Suzy I don't know, but -

LIL walks into the frame. Suzy, quickly takes her mail cart and leaves

                        LIL
        I just found this letter from Eastern U. - they inquire why
        Tom hadn't responded to their terms of employment. Did
        you know of any such overtures?

                        ANNE
        Never heard of any job offer.

                        LIL
        If one has a suspicious mind - you know - one could assume
        Tom was ready to sell out our longevity concept to Eastern...
        No, he wouldn't do that.

The telephone rings. ANNE picks up

                        ANNE
        South Coast College, Dr. Johnson's office.

ANNE listens for a while. She is uneasy.

                         ANNE
              Well - -

ANNE covers the receiver with her hand. She looks up at LIL

                         ANNE
              Kevin - I mean Detective McGuire wants me to have lunch
              with him...

                         LIL
              Why not? What's wrong with that? He seems to be an OK
              guy.

                         ANNE
              I'm a recent widow. I can't go on a date, just yet.

                         LIL
              You'll have lunch with him. Big deal. You don't jump into bed
              with him. Come on - accept.

ANNE picks up receiver

                         ANNE
              Kevin - - yes - - glad to - - "Wheel and Anchor" - twelve
              thirty -

                         LIL
              That wasn't so hard, was it.

                         ANNE
              No, but- -

                         LIL
              That Kevin McGuire is quite a hunk. I could go for him
              myself.

(NOTE: Forward movement Main Plot: Suzy is worried about Shawn. Lil's remark about
Easter University's letter. Forward movement Sub Plot: Kevin invites Anne.)

<u>INTERIOR "WHEEL AND ANCHOR" DINING ROOM. DAY</u>
ANNE and Kevin are seated at a window table. There is consistent movement as people come
and go, a waiter refills their cups, etc.

                         KEVIN
              ...don't give Catherine another thought.

ANNE

I don't know. There is some connection between her and
Bob, and now she's after Shawn. Get it?

KEVIN

Catherine's a cradle snatcher.

ANNE

How about Suzy's suspicion that Catherine recruits for one of
Sven's - I suspect - more advanced seminars?

KEVIN

A secret one?

ANNE

Possibly.

KEVIN

One that is not listed in the college catalog?

ANNE

You've got it. A seminar that calls for a - kind of special
student.

KEVIN

Got you. I bet there's something weird going on behind
South Coast's pristine, ivy covered walls.

ANNE

Could be... By the way, remember you'd asked me whether
Tom had received any employment offers.

KEVIN

Right.

ANNE

This morning Lil showed me a letter that indicated Eastern
University had offered him a job.

KEVIN

Was Tom ready to cash in on whatever he knew about
longevity -

ANNE

How should I know, Tom never confided in me.

KEVIN
Sven was afraid that Tom might sell out. Bingo. He killed
him. It makes sense.

ANNE
Get a search warrant and move in on Sven's secret lab.

Eagerly ANNE leans forward.

KEVIN
I can't. I need evidence to justify a warrant.

ANNE
I know. You've told me

KEVIN
Right. But I'll gun for Sven. I promise you. Eventually I'll
wear him down and bring him to justice. He killed Tom. I am
sure of it.

Comforting KEVIN cradles ANNE'S hands in his.

KEVIN
You'll have to help me. Please. Talk to people I might have
trouble meeting. People who distrust me.

His fingers tighten around ANNE's hand.

KEVIN
I hope you won't mind.

ANNE looks at him.

KEVIN
We'll have to spend much time together.

CU on KEVIN's hands covering her hands. Reluctantly, but deliberately she pulls her hand
away.

Back on ANNE and KEVIN.

ANNE
I'll do whatever is necessary for you to prove that Tom was
murdered, but -

A sense of relief mingled with sadness surges through ANNE

                         ANNE
          - but - I won't meet you anymore in places like this
          restaurant. If I should find out something I'll call or come to
          your office. San Louis is a small town. People talk. And I
          don't want your wife to get the wrong idea.

                         KEVIN
          I'm not married.

(NOTE: Forward movement Main Plot: Possibly Tom was killed because he sold out Sven's
longevity research. Kevin is ready to go after Sven. Forward Movement Sub-Plot: Anne's and
Kevin's growing attraction)

ESTABLISHING SHOT. SVEN'S HILLSIDE HOUSE. NIGHT.
Ultra modern. Huge glass windows. Redwood trim. A flat tile roof.

INTERIOR SVEN'S HOME. LIVING ROOM. NIGHT.
Everything - from the build in bookcases, leather couches and wire framed chairs - is depress-
ingly functional. The whitewashed walls give the room an antiseptic air. Sven's domicil may as
well be a laboratory. Bleak but fascinating.

ANNE, looking for LIL, makes her way through the festive crowd. Faculty and a few "selected"
students are gathered to celebrate SVEN'S birthday. ANNE passes by SVEN and Dr. MICHNER

                         SVEN
          You are South Coast's president - Dr. Michner.

                       DR. MICHNER
          All right, my good fellow, but -

ANNE'S POV. CATHERINE has her arms around SHAWN. She whispers something.
SHAWN a bit embarrassed, laughs. SUZY, watching the two, pouts in a corner.

ANNE walks up to LIL and FATHER O'BRIAN

                         LIL
          - - one of the experiments, he and Sven worked on.

LIL turns to ANNE
                         LIL
          Good to see you.

LIL turns back to the priest.

                         LIL
          Anyway Tom was bound and determined to proof that a rat
          was able to take over the soul -

The priest, smilingly, raises a warning finger.

> LIL
>
> Sorry - personality of an alien creature. Well, Sven kept this king snake in his private lab -

> ANNE
>
> Here...in this house?

> LIL
>
> Why sure, Sven's special experiments are all conducted in his playroom - sorry, his lab. Well, anyway, Tom put the revived rat in a cage with a King-snake -

> ANNE
>
> Revived? Do you mean the rat had been killed before the experiment took place?

> LIL
>
> 'Course what else? Nearly killed and then revived.

> ANNE
>
> Did Tom ever suggest that similar experiments were done on...let's say...human subjects?

Lil laughs

> LIL
>
> Don't tell me you're afraid Sven asked one of his students to share the cage with a snake?

> ANNE
>
> No. But was it ever considered that human beings might become more resilient, or -

LIL, her voice caressing, takes the priest's arm -

> LIL
>
> Father I want you meet someone...

- and walks off. ANNE turns. She makes her way through the living room to a door.

(NOTE: Forward movement Main Plot: A lab is located in Sven's house. Obviously strange experiments are taking place. Question 6: Will Anne find evidence of such experiments?)

<u>INTERIOR SVEN's HOME. HALLWAY. NIGHT.</u>
ANNE hurries through the hallway. She opens a door, looks into a kitchen. Quickly she closes the door, and hurries on, opens another door .

ANNE's POV, a staircase leading downstairs.

ANNE descends the stairs.

INTERIOR SVEN'S HOUSE. BASEMENT. HALLWAY. NIGHT
Another hallway. Lights seeps in through a high set basement window. ANNE walks to a door.

She hesitates for a moment, then taking a deep breath, she reaches for the doorknob. There is another moment of hesitation before she opens the door.

INTERIOR SVEN'S HOUSE. LAB. NIGHT.
Moonlight, dimly illuminates the room. ANNE enters, she looks around.

ANNE'S POV. A Bunsen burner and some empty cages are stashed in the corner.
Back on ANNE disappointed. She is ready to leave. The sound of a car passing by, makes her look up. Headlights flash.

ANNE's POV. The car's headlights flash across a freezer's steel door.

Back on ANNE. She tenses.

ANNE's POV. The freezer. Ominous. Threatening.

Back on ANNE. She calls herself to order, walks up to the freezer. Hesitates. Afraid to open the freezer, she is ready to leave.

ANNE'S POV. The door - leading from the hallway to the lab - opens a crack.

BACK on ANNE. Without making a sound, she opens the freezer's door and slips inside.

INSIDE FREEZER. Something hits ANNE. A moment of panic before she discovers a broom handle has landed on her shoulder. The threatening freezer turns out to be a broom closet.

ANNE'S POV. Mops, another broom, some buckets. SOUND OVER: someone dialing a phone number.

                    DR. MICHNER (VO)
           Darling, so sorry. I couldn't...

BACK on ANNE. Smiling to herself she opens the freezer door a crack

ANNE'S POV. Dr. Michner on the phone.

                    DR. MICHNER
           - call you earlier, but you know how suspicious my wife is... I
           have to keep up my reputation. Don't forget I'm South
           Coast's president. The community looks up to me. Yes, I'll
           see you tomorrow. Can't wait to hold -

Back on Dr. MICHNER

DR. MICHNER
- to hold you in my arms. And wear that cute little, lacy
thing - whatever it is.

Dr. Michner blows a kiss. Smiling, happy with himself he hangs up and leaves. ANNE exits the freezer.

(NOTE: Question 6 answered: Nothing in Sven's lab points to criminal experiments. RED HERRING, misinformation.)

INTERIOR SVEN'S HOUSE. BASEMENT. HALLWAY. NIGHT.
ANNE hurries through the hallway. A sudden, swishing sound makes her stop and listen. ANNE'S POV. A squirrel darts from behind some crates.

INTERIOR SVEN's HOUSE LIVING ROOM. NIGHT.
ANNE mingles with the guests.

ANNE's POV. SVEN grabs LIL by her shoulders. Furiously she shakes herself loose,

LIL
You no good, ungrateful...

LIL runs to the door. Sven hurries after her, but then changing his mind, he shrugs his shoulders, and returns to his guests.

INTERIOR VICTORIAN MANSION. ANNE'S BEDROOM. NIGHT.
On ANNE asleep. The telephone rings. ANNE turns, she keeps on sleeping. SOUND OVER: grandfather clock in the hallway striking three, the telephone shrills again. ANNE wakes up, still groggy with sleep she pick up the phone.

ANNE
Lil?

INTERCUT ANNE and LIL on the phones

LIL
Come over right away. It's all my fault.

ANNE
What's your fault?

A racking sob answers.

LIL
I shouldn't have left him alone.

ANNE
Make some sense.

LIL
Sven - someone killed him.

(NOTE: Main Plot forward movement. Sven was killed. Surprise. Question 7: Who killed Sven.)

EXTERIOR SVEN'S HOUSE. NIGHT
Bedlam. The street is blocked off with yellow tape. ANNE and LIL, on their way to the front door pass a TV crew, police cars, the coroner's van. A police officer guards the front door. LIL identifies herself, before she and ANNE enter the house.

INTERIOR SVEN'S HOUSE. LIVING ROOM. NIGHT.
On SVEN's body sprawled on the floor. A police photographer takes photos while two forensic experts do their job, two or three police officers stand around. Quickly ANNE maneuvers LIL to a corner where Kevin talks to a reporter.

REPORTER (taking notes)
Any sings of struggle -

KEVIN
As far as we know - none.

REPORTER
Evidence of forcible entry?

KEVIN
None.

REPORTER
That means the victim might have known the assailant?

KEVIN
Could be.

Reporter flips a page in his notebook

REPORTER
Anything missing?

KEVIN
Gimme a break, Bill. We've been here a little over an hour.
How much can we find out in such a short time.

REPORTER
There are rumors that Dr. Johnson worked on a highly provocative research. Any possible connection between this project and the murder?

KEVIN
So far Dr. Johnson's murder has not been connected to his research.

REPORTER
Whatever you say.

REPORTER hurries away. ANNE and LIL watch the coroner's crew strap the corpse on a stretcher.

LIL
Eastern U. is to blame. They hired a killer to do their dirty work. They killed Sven. And they killed Tom.

ANNE
Wait a moment - you agree that Tom was murdered?

LIL
I do - - finally - - let's go.

ANNE wrapping her arm around LIL, steers her to the front door.

LIL
Longevity has moved from hypothesis to theory. Can you imagine the feather in Eastern U.'s cap, if they - not Sven - had grown the longevity research on their own turf.

ANNE
Get off it. Longevity is not that unique. A number of scientists travel down the same road, I know, Tom told me.

ANNE and LIL have reached the front door. A police officer opens the door for them. They exit.

EXTERIOR SVEN'S HOUSE. DAWN.
Passing the corner's van and police cars, LIL and ANNE walk to ANNE'S car.

LIL
True. And the more ethical ones of the research labs buy out some dumb jerk who has spend all his life, and strength, and money developing a project. Tom - if I am not mistaken -

By now they have reached ANNE's car. ANNE digs in her purse for her keys.

                              LIL
          - was ready to talk, but backed out. That's why they took care
          of him. Then they went after Sven. But that guy had his
          mind set on the Nobel Prize. He craved the glory and the
          laurels. He'd never sell out. So, get rid of Johnson, steal the
          research papers.

                              ANNE
          But we don't know yet whether anything's missing. Remem-
          ber Kevin said -

                              LIL
          How dumb can you be. There's microfilm. Someone had
          plenty of time.

ANNE's POV, on the coroner's van driving off.

                           LIL (V.O.)
          Eastern U. is nothing but a bunch of thieves and killers.

Move in on turning wheels

                           LIL (V.O.)
          I'm going to nail them.

(NOTE: Surprise: Sven's murder. Forward movement Main Plot: It seems that Tom was involved in industrial spying. By now the audience in convinced that Eastern University is behind
Sven's and possibly Tom's murder. RED HERRING.)

INTERIOR SUPERMARKET. DAY
CU on shopping cart's wheels. PULL OUT. ANNE pushes a shopping cart. LIL walks next to
her.

                              ANNE
          Any success in nailing Eastern U?

                              LIL
          Nothing.

                              ANNE
          What did you expect?

They stop in front of "fruits and vegetables". ANNE reaches for a head of lettuce, checks it's
firmness, puts it in her cart, counts some tomatoes in a plastic bag

                              LIL
          Dr. Michner our beloved leader, that pompous ass threatened
          to fire me if I were to take action against Eastern U.

ANNE weighs the bag.

                    ANNE
        I'm not surprised, Kevin is convinced -

                    LIL
        How about that handsome hunk of a guy?

                    ANNE
    Come on

                    LIL
        Let me tell you, that guy's falling for you

ANNE and LIL move on to another aisle.

                    ANNE
        Kevin is a good friend, nothing more.

                    LIL
    Don't fool yourself.

                    ANNE
        All right, I'm - kind of - attracted to him

                    LIL
        Makes sense. That guy is different from Tom

                    ANNE
        But I feel guilty about - well - liking Kevin.

Again they stop. ANNE adds a few cans of soup to her purchases

                    ANNE
        Tom passed on just a short while ago. I have no right to - well
        yes, - feel something for another man.

                    LIL
        If I were you I'd grab that Kevin guy. But it's your choice.
        Anyway I've got to run. Got to teach that boring Psych class
        old Michner settled me with. See you later alligator-

                    ANNE
        And don't smile at a crocodile

LIL hurries of. ANNE reaches for another can of soup.

ANNE's POV. Wearing a loud Hawaiian shirt, and disguised by a cap, a MAN blocks the aisle

ANNE
Excuse me.

ANNE moves to the next aisle. She reaches for a box of cereal. Again the MAN intently watching her - this time standing closer - blocks the aisle. ANNE now uneasy, makes her way to the check out counter.

ANNE places her purchases on the conveyer belt. And again the MAN stands close, this time he browses through the magazine rack.

ANNE watches him out of the corner of her eyes. Suddenly the MAN looks straight at her, he takes his cap off -

ANNE
Bob...

PULL in on BOB. PULL in closer on his comatose, nearly fish like unexpressive eyes. Quickly, forgetting her purchases, ANNE walks up to him

ANNE
Bob...

BOB turns and runs out of the supermarket

ANNE
Bob - Bob - Wait - Wait -

(NOTE: Forward movement Main Plot: Anne sees a very much alive Bob. Forward movement Sub Plot: Anne admits she loves Kevin)

EXTERIOR PARKING LOT. DAY.
Skirting cars, always yelling his name ANNE chases BOB.

RESIDENTIAL STREET DAY
BOB runs across a street, and down the sidewalk of a residential street bordered by small Victorian cottages. The old street, completely devoid of life breathes the surrealistic unreality of a nightmare.

Several takes on BOB running, and ANNE following him.

Unexpectedly BOB stops in front of a Victorian cottage. Some of the windows are boarded up, the front yard is overgrown with weeds. With a stiff, almost mechanical movement, BOB reaches for the door knob.

ANNE
Bob - wait for me.

A blinding flash, the agonizing screech of brakes. A car, almost hitting her, throws ANNE to the side. She falls to the ground, presses her fingers against the pavement.

After a while, still shaking, ANNE scrambles to her feet. She dusts off her jeans, looks around. ANNE's POV, BOB is nowhere to be seen.

ANNE walks up to the cottage. She opens the door and enters.

INTERIOR VICTORIAN COTTAGE. HALLWAY. DAY
The narrow hallway is littered with debris and broken glass. Streamers of torn wallpaper cover the walls.

                              ANNE
                   Bob...

No answer. ANNE opens a door.

ANNE's POV: the equally dismal parlor. A fireplace, partially hidden by a stack of crates. The room is covered with dust and dirt.

Back on ANNE. She opens another door.

ANNE'S POV. A narrow staircase leading to the basement.

Back on ANNE Quickly she closes the door. She hurries through the hallway to the back porch.

EXTERIOR VICTORIAN COTTAGE. BACK PORCH. DAY.
ANNE rushes out to the back porch. All of a sudden she stops, freezes. Her POV. SVEN's house rising a short distance above the cottage. Above the house, the "shelter" a curious, partially torn down shack, crouches into the mountain side.

Motionless ANNE stares at the shelter.

(NOTE: Forward movement Main Plot: The location of the three buildings provides Anne with a clue as to the secret lab's possible location)

EXTERIOR "SHELTER". DAY.
ANNE and KEVIN climb up a steep, rocky hill.

                              ANNE
              I'm telling you I saw Bob at the little cottage down there.

                              KEVIN
              Forget about Bob. I'm sure you made the same mistake Mr.
              McGowan made... I wish that women would stop pestering
              us with her "sightings".

KEVIN, catching his breath, stops for a moment.

                              KEVIN
              You saw someone who looked a bit like Bob.

They have arrived at the entrance to the "shelter". KEVIN surveys the location. He nods.

> KEVIN
>
> That squirrel -

> ANNE
>
> I've found in Sven's basement.

> KEVIN
>
> Could've possibly sneaked in through here. I'm telling you, you came up with something significant. Did you know -

Slowly the camera pans from the shelter to SVEN's house, and from there to the cottage.

> KEVIN (V.O.)
>
> Did you know, the Victorian cottages down there are built upon the foundations of mid 19th century adobe buildings. Anyway, the early settlers were afraid of outlaws. So, they fortified their homes with basements from which a network of tunnels...

Back on KEVIN AND ANNE

> KEVIN
>
> - led to the hills and safety.

KEVIN, love in his eyes, looks at ANNE

> KEVIN
>
> There's something I wanted to say. Well, I don't know how to say it. But you and I -

Unable to express his feelings, KEVIN stops before he takes another plunge.

> KEVIN
>
> You are still grieving for Tom, and I have no right - -

Uneasily without looking at KEVIN, ANNE interrupts

> ANNE
>
> I bet the squirrel came through one of these tunnels. Maybe the tunnel's entrance is right here at the shelter, and some-where -

ANNE points to the line of houses

ANNE's POV. Two cars maneuver up the steep road. They stop in front of Sven's house

ANNE (V.O.)
- between the tunnel, possibly in the cottage that's where we will find -

LIL, CATHERINE and DR. MICHNER exit one of the cars.

Back on KEVIN and ANNE

KEVIN
Let me get it off my chest, I've got to say it...

ANNE
The entrance to the tunnel...and Sven's secret lab.

KEVIN
Sorry, I've shouldn't have...forget what I said.

KEVIN'S POV. Two men in business suits exit the second car.

KEVIN (V.O.)
I know these two characters. They are with the FBI

Back on ANNE and KEVIN.

KEVIN
Something is wrong. Let's take a look.

(NOTE: Forward movement Sub Plot: Kevin tries to tell Anne he loves her. Question 8: What is the FBI after)

INTERIOR SVEN'S HOUSE. LIVING ROOM. DAY
The FBI has turned the living room upside down. Bookcases and desk drawers stand open. The floor is covered with Sven's research papers. The FBI agents, searching for any hidden recess, pound the walls. Calmly LIL watches. KEVIN and ANNE enter.

Dr. MICHNER glares at LIL

DR. MICHNER
Dr. Stanhope, let me ask you again what is it you are trying to cover up?

LIL
I'm not covering up a darn thing.

LIL turns to ANNE and KEVIN

LIL
Join the fun.

ANNE sits down next to LIL. She put a calming hand on her friend's arm. KEVIN flashes his badge.

                              KEVIN
              Detective McGuire, San Louis police department.

KEVIN picks up some of the papers littering the floor.

                            FBI AGENT I
              Fingerprints, watch it.

                              KEVIN
              You're leaving quite a few of your own. Anyway, why not let
              me know what you're after. Maybe I can help.

                            FBI AGENT II
              We have orders to search for Dr. Johnson's secret lab.

                               LIL
              Preposterous. Dr. Michner I can't understand why you permit
              this farce.

                           DR. MICHNER
              I am South Coast's president. I'm doing my duty. Dr. Gerard
              made some - shall I say - leading remarks regarding Dr.
              Johnson's research.

                              ANNE
              Tom? What did my husband say?

                           DR. MICHNER
              He mentioned human experiments.

LIL whispers to ANNE

                               LIL
              Don't listen to that pompous ass.

She turns to DR. MICHNER and the FBI agents.

                               LIL
              No one has any proof about anything Tom might, or might
              not have said. I bet, this tempest in a tea pot is nothing but
              the result of some stupid accusations Eastern U. fabricated.

                           DR. MICHNER
              The FBI would not be here if Eastern University's accusations
              were unfounded.

                    FBI AGENT I
        We have a signed statement from a Mrs. McGowen to the
        effect that one of her borders -

KEVIN shakes his head. He laughs.

                      KEVIN
        Bob. Mrs. McGowen at her best.

The two FBI AGENTS favor KEVIN with haughty looks

                    FBI AGENT II
        - mentioned experiments conducted on humans.

                      KEVIN
        May I remind you that it was I who took the aforementioned
        statement. You, gentlemen, can pound the walls of this room
        until doomsday, and I bet...

KEVIN exchanges a look with ANNE

                      KEVIN
        - you won't find this blasted secret lab.

                       LIL
        Regardless of what - let me put it mildly -

LIL walks to the room's wood panelled, white painted walls.

                       LIL
        - some overly imaginative individuals might have conjured,
        Sven never conducted any criminal experiments. The secret
        lab, however, does exist.

LIL pushes an almost invisible button. The paneling slides aside. LIL points to a small en-
closed shelve that contains a few file cabinets. LIL opens one of the file cabinets and reaches for
a folder.
                       LIL
        Here is Sven's secret lab. His life work.

On KEVIN, the FBI AGENTS and DR. MICHNER, amazed, speechless. DR. MICHNER,
as not to be outdone, turns to the FBI AGENTS.

                   DR. MICHNER
        Longevity. Dr. Johnson published some highly provocative
        articles on this topic.

                              LIL
          You're wrong, The documents deal with...immortality.

A gasp goes through the room. No one dares to speak.

                              LIL
          If Sven had lived to conclude his research...

LIL gazes at he folders, then she turns to Dr. MICHNER.

                              LIL
          I entrust these files to you. I assure you, you won't find
          anything unethical or criminal in Sven's research.

                             KEVIN
          Wait a minute. Legally this research -

KEVIN steps in front of the file cabinet

                             KEVIN
          - is still Sven's property. Not until his estate has been settled,
          can his research -

                          DR. MICHNER
          I appreciate the legal complications.

DR. MICHNER turns to LIL.

                          DR. MICHNER
          But perhaps Dr. Stanhope might give us some hint about the
          research's general scope, it's basic concept, and -

                              LIL
          Gladly.

                         FBI AGENT I
          In lay terms, if you don't mind.

During the following explanation camera moves back and forth between LIL, KEVIN,
DR. MICHNER, CATHERINE and the two FBI Agents.

                            LIL
Sven believed that life could go on forever. He looked upon
aging as a form of disease that should be cured. In other
words, he did not believe in the genetic clock. Aging begins
when the DNA code fails to send the message to repair itself.
If we can correct this process then cells will not age. Another
hypotheses contents that a number of genes - possibly one
gene only - lead the system to death. If - sometimes in the
future - we will be able to combine the two hypothesis to
form a theory, humans may achieve immortality.

                       DR. MICHNER
Life ever lasting.

The two FBI AGENTS look at each other, KEVIN sighs, LIL raises her hand.

                            LIL
Please understand at this point we are decades away from -

The front door flies open. SUZY storms into the room. She grabs CATHERINE and slaps her
across the face.

                           SUZY
You bitch, you filthy bitch. Where's Shawn?

KEVIN pulls SUZY away from CATHERINE. SUZY, a bundle of misery curls up on the
floor. ANNE kneels next to her. Comforting she strokes the girls hair. SUZY sobs.

                           SUZY
Shawn...He told me about some experiments that Catherine
wanted him to participate in, but I talked him out. Everything was going great between him and me. We wanted to
look for my engagement ring yesterday. He never showed up.

A burst of venom directed at LIL.

                           SUZY
She killed him for her shitty experiments. I know. And
Catherine that bitch helped her.

(NOTE: Question 8 answered: The FBI is after the secret lab. Main Plot forward movement:
No criminal experiments took place .RED HERRING. Sven worked on the immortality, not
longevity concept. SURPRISE. Suzy accuses Lil of conducting criminal experiments)

<u>INTERIOR MCGOWEN BOARDING HOUSE. MRS. MCGOWEN'S LIVING ROOM.
DAY.</u>

Mrs. MCGOWEN'S red plush nightmare of a living room. Excitedly, garments flowing, Mrs.
MCGOWEN walks around the room. ANNE watches her.

MRS. MCGOWEN
I knew it. I knew it. First Bob, now Shawn. I feel it in my bones, something mighty strange's going on.

ANNE
Detective McGuire said -

MRS. MCGOWEN
Forget about the cops. Them won't do a darn thing. It's up to you and me, hon, to stick our noses into the dirt.

MRS. MCGOWEN pulls a paper from the pocket.

Mrs. MCGOWEN
Found this when I cleaned up Bob's room. A receipt for flowers delivered in Catherine's name to a Mrs. Garber. Lives in a rest home somewhere out in the country,

ANNE
A rest home? I can't see any connection. A rest home has nothing to do with either Bob's or Shawn's disappearance.

MRS. MCGOWEN
Don't you get it? Rest home - old people-some die - some could be used for experiments. You know, helped into eternity. Guinea pigs.

ANNE
You mean, no one asks, no one cares.

MRS. MCGOWEN
Guinea pigs.

ANNE
Some atrocity...at the nursing home.

MRS. MCGOWEN
And Bob and that Catherine are involved.

(NOTE: Forward movement Main Plot: CATHERINE has some connections to a nursing home)

EXTERIOR NURSING HOME. DAY.
A plain but well kept building.

INTERIOR NURSING HOME. MRS. GARBER'S ROOM. DAY.
A small room. Friendly. Compact. The window stands wide open. The walls are plastered with photos. Mrs. Garber, a feisty old lady, cackles -

MRS. GARBER
- hundred years old. Would ye believe it?

ANNE
You surely don't look it

MRS. GARBER
Have seen more stupid things than I like to remember. Yep -
I'm hundred years old.

ANNE scans the walls. Her POV, prominently displayed over some framed newspaper articles, she notices CATHERINE'S photo.

MRS. GARBER (V.O.)
They all came to my birthday, the newspapers, the people from -

Back on ANNE and MRS. GARBER

MRS. GARBER
- how ye call it?

ANNE
TV?

ANNE points to CATHERINE'S photo

ANNE
You have a beautiful great- granddaughter.

MRS. GARBER
Great- granddaughter did ye say?

ON CATHERINE's photo.

MRS. GARBER (V.O.)
- that kid's my daughter, my -

Back an ANNE and MRS. GARBER. The old woman, emphasizing every word pounds the floor with her cane.

MRS. GARBER
-daughter - ye hear - my daughter.

The door flies open. MELINDA, a nurse, enters. She carries a tea tray.

MELINDA
Calm down Aunt Harriet, everything is all right.

MELINDA sets down the tea tray, pours a cup of tea and hands MRS. GARBER a cookie.

> MELINDA
> Snatched some Milans for you. Enjoy.

Unexpectedly MELINDA grabs ANNE's arm, whispers -

> MELINDA
> Want to talk to you, Missy.

MELINDA turns back to MRS. GARBER -

> MELINDA
> Enjoy your tea.

- and propels ANNE out of the room.

INTERIOR NURSING HOME. HALLWAY. DAY

> MELINDA
> I was out on the terrace. I've heard what you said. No one
> here ever mentions Cathy.

> ANNE
> Sorry, I didn't know.

> MELINDA
> Don't give me any excuses. Just tell me who you are and what
> you want.

MELINDA, hovering over ANNE, is frightening.

> MELINDA
> Cat got your tongue? Come on. Answer me. Can't wait all
> day.

> ANNE
> I'm Anne Gerard. Mrs. Gerard.

MELINDA's expression softens.

> MELINDA
> Gerard? That name rings a bell. Your husband taught
> somewhere.

> ANNE
> South Coast College in San Louis.

MELINDA
And the poor guy died recently. I've read it in the paper. He
was involved in some newfangled research, wasn't he?

ANNE
My husband worked on the longevity project.

MELINDA
That's what they call it now?

Poorly disguised hatred flares in MELINDA's eyes. But then she extends her hand.

MELINDA
I'm Melinda Garber, Aunt Harriet's grand niece.

There's a short but awkward pause. A orderly pushes a lunch wagon along the hallway.

ORDERLY
'Cuse me.

Slowly MELINDA and ANNE make their way along the hallway to a door leading outside.

MELINDA
Your husband worked for Sven Johnson? That's what the
paper indicated.

ANNE
They worked together...Sven was murdered.

MELINDA
He had it coming.

Startled by the look of vindictive satisfaction on MELINDA'S face, ANNE cautiously goes on.

ANNE
We have a Catherine Garber working at South Coast...that's
why I'm here.

MELINDA looks at ANNE she's ready to say something, but shrugs.

MELINDA
Probably a woman who has the same name my grand aunt
has. Garber isn't an unusual name. Catherine Garber, Aunt
Harriet's daughter vanished fifty years ago.

ANNE
I'm not speaking about an old lady. I'm speaking about a
woman in her middle-twenties.

MELINDA
So, the bastard succeeded after all.

ANNE
Who succeeded in what -

MELINDA
Forget what I've just said.

ANNE
You better tell me.

MELINDA
All right. But let's go outside. I don' want anyone to overhear us.

ANNE and MELINDA walk to the door, they exit.

EXTERIOR REST HOME. GROUNDS. DAY.
On ANNE and MELINDA walking along.

MELINDA
Catherine is Aunt Harriet's daughter. Catherine was born in 1925.

ANNE
Impossible

MELINDA
That's what I'm saying. She vanished...in a way...

They stop at a small fountain. Water, leisurely, trickles into a stone basin. The peaceful setting stands in stark contrast to the women's dialog.

MELINDA
Let me tell you about Catherine - Cathy we called her. She was different from the rest of us. More inquisitive, more eager to plunge into any adventure. She worked as a nurse in our hospital. Made friends with a group of interns. One of them was Sven Johnson. Catherine told us he worked on something called "Ever lasting youth."

ANNE
Longevity

MELINDA
Whatever. Catherine got all caught up in the craziness.

MELINDA, suddenly cold, wraps her arms around her shoulders.

On the fountain.

                    MELINDA (V.O.)
          Sven and Catherine took off to some small mountain resort -

Back on ANNE and MELINDA

                    MELINDA
          - forgot the name - when Catherine returned, she had
          changed. She...was cold.

                    ANNE
          Physically or emotionally -

                    MELINDA
          Both. A few weeks later Catherine left. We never know where
          she is. She doesn't write doesn't call, only ever so often sends
          those   sick flower baskets...It's eery...

                    ANNE
          What do you think happened to her?

                    MELINDA
          Something bizarre, I think -

                    ANNE
          What do you think

                    MELINDA
          Sven killed her.

                    ANNE
          That doesn't make any sense.

                    MELINDA
          Well, I mean he didn't outright murder her. Catherine's body
          is alive. I can't explain it. Something in Cathy is dead...her
          spirit...her soul is gone...He turned her into some -

MELINDA struggles for words

                    MELINDA
          - some...some kind of a living dead.

(NOTE. HIGHLIGHT SCENE. Forward movement Main Plot: Because of Sven's experiment Catherine remains young forever. TWIST.)

<u>EXTERIOR OCEAN. KEVIN'S BOAT DAY</u>
A bright, sunny day. KEVIN and ANNE sailing.

> KEVIN
> Ridiculous. Don't get caught in that woman's science fiction fantasy.

KEVIN reaches out for ANNE's hands.

> KEVIN
> I've got to tell you something. Please hear me out. I know I have no right to say this -

KEVIN hesitates before he goes on.

> KEVIN
> - but...here it goes...I love you.

ANNE looks into KEVIN's eyes. Love and commitment speak to her. She kisses KEVIN

(NOTE. Forward movement Sub-Plot: Kevin and Anne admit their love for each other.)

<u>INTERIOR VICTORIAN MANSION. LIVING ROOM. NIGHT</u>

ANNE on the phone. Books are all over the floor. A floor lamp, next to the desk, dimly lights the room.

> ANNE
> - cleaning out the bookshelves.

ANNE reaches for a book.

> ANNE
> The parish has another book sale. I promised Father O'Brian some books - no...nothing sexy...of course not...You've got night duty...Don't work too hard.

ANNE listens for a moment. An inner glow lights up her face.

> ANNE
> Yes...I love you too...see you tomorrow.

ANNE hangs up, she stretches, stakes the books, picks up one book. Uncertain whether or not to keep it, she sits down on a wing chair, starts reading but dozes off. The hallway clock strikes. Demanding, booming sounds shatter the room's stillness.

ANNE forces herself to open her eyes. She shivers, seems to get colder and colder. She tries to reach for the blanket next to her but is unable to move.

And now intermingling with the booming clock sounds, drifts a love song through the room...louder and louder ... the love song changes to a voice spitting out epitaphs...then, making the walls shake, hard rock blasts around ANNE.

Birds began to chirp...screech...then merge with the cacophony resounding through the room.

Now - all of a sudden - silence. Hammering, threatening silence. ANNE, using all her willpower, moves her head slightly.

ANNE's POV. Two bluish orbs of light float some five feet above the floor. The orbs, quivering close to each other, expand until they are about the size of tennis balls.

Back on ANNE eyes riveted on the orbs. All strength seeps away from her as streaks of light flash from her chest.

ANNE'S POV. The two orbs merge into one single, larger orb, that - elongating to an oblong shape of wavering lights - quickly expand to human size.

Back on ANNE. She forces herself to remain calm.

ANNE'S POV. For a few seconds there is nothing but this luminous glow, then - slowly - the glow turns into a human shape. Human features emerge.

Back on ANNE. She screams, a long hallow sound.

ANNE's POV. Tom emerges where the oblong shape had wavered.

A very human, watchful expression in his eyes he looks at her.

BACK on ANNE Her screams turning into whimpers, she looks at that -thing - that looks like Tom.

ANNE's POV. Tom, floating, moves closer and closer.

Back on ANNE. Laboriously, slowly, using all her strength, her eyes riveted on TOM. ANNE pushes herself up. She slides off the chair. While the room reverberates with bird cries, hard rock blares into her ears, ANNE moves to the door, opens the door, exits and slams the door shut.

INTERIOR VICTORIAN MANSION. UPPER HALLWAY. NIGHT.
ANNE runs through the hallway to the staircase, stumbles down the stairs.

INTERIOR VICTORIAN MANSION. ENTRANCE HALLWAY. NIGHT.
ANNE throws the front door open and escapes.

<u>EXTERIOR VICTORIAN MANSION. NIGHT.</u>
ANNE breathless, runs out of the house. She catches her breath, starts running again. Now the birds are all around her. Wings flutter, bills peck at her face. In an attempt to fight off her attackers, ANNE huddles next to her car. Keeping her eyes closed, she covers her head with both hands.

Suddenly, unexpectedly the birds are gone. Everything is quiet. ANNE listens. After a while she opens her eyes, looks around.

ANNE'S POV. Front yard, the Victorian looms like a threatening shadow.

Back on ANNE With difficulty, holding on to the car, she pulls herself up. She tries to open the car door. The car is locked. And then the birds - shrieking, pecking - are back. ANNE starts running.

<u>EXTERIOR STREET. NIGHT.</u>
A dark, narrow lane, dimly illuminated by moonlight. Stumbling, exhausted ANNE keeps running, down the street and around a corner. A hand grabs ANNE's shoulder, holds her back, almost forces her to the ground.

ANNE rounds a corner, when the hand - this disembodied hand - pushes against her chest. There is no air to breath. ANNE gasps. Chokes.

Everything revolves around her. The night's darkness closes in on her.

<u>INTERIOR VICARAGE. NIGHT.</u>
It is obvious Father O'BRIAN has worked on his sermon, the computer is lit, papers litter his desk, a stack of books is piled on the window sill.

ANNE huddles near the fireplace. The priest busies himself at the coffeepot

ANNE
I still don't know how I got here.

FATHER O'BRIAN
You rang the doorbell like a maniac. Must have woken up the
whole neighborhood... Sugar, Cream?

ANNE
Cream only, please.

FATHER O'BRIAN hands ANNE a mug. Gratefully ANNE cradles her hands around the mug's welcome warmth.

ANNE
What I told you, about what happened to me, must have
sounded like the rambling of a demented mind.

                    FATHER O'BRIAN
        On the contrary. I do believe in ghostly appearances.

Realizing her experience had indeed been real brings the terror back. ANNE begins
to shake. The coffee spills on the floor.

                         ANNE
              Sorry.

                    FATHER O'BRIAN
        Don't worry about spilled beans - or in our case, spilled
        coffee.

The priest takes the mug. He hands ANNE a blanket. Gratefully, still shaking, she cuddles into
the blanket.
                         ANNE
              You believe in ghosts?

                    FATHER O'BRIAN
        I do. Man is a far more dynamic creature than science credits
        him with.

The priest pours some coffee.

                    FATHER O'BRIAN
        So far the logical mind has not even touched the acceptance
        of an invisible world surrounding us. Yet non-physical
        entities - and the Church never -

As the priest turns and walks over to Anne and hands her the mug, the room's atmosphere
slightly changes. A faint, hardly discernible reddish glow spreads throughout the room.

                    FATHER O'BRIAN
        - denied it...do exist independently from human being. So
        far science - reluctantly - accepted the fact of an energy aura
        vibrating around every living thing, man, plant and animal.

A sudden reddish glow distorts the priests face to a mask.

                    FATHER O'BRIAN
        This, to the human eye invisible luminescent glow is created
        by the body's energy discharge.

Slowly the reddish glow diminishes. The room's atmosphere returns to normal.

                    FATHER O'BRIAN
        Thoughts are energy related, so are feelings, fears and desires.
        There is a good chance that thought patterns keep ghosts
        earthbound.

                           ANNE
              Are you speaking about Tom's research?

                       FATHER O'BRIAN
              Possibly.

EXTERIOR CONDO. DAY.
ANNE and KEVIN walk up to the condo.

                           KEVIN
              - your "quote" visions were nothing but a nightmare -

Playfully ANNE pushes him aside, she laughs

                           ANNE
              Come on. Be serious. That house, believe me, is creepesville.
              Anyway I've decided to rent a room at Mrs. McGowen for a
              while.

                           KEVIN
              That police prosecuting witch? Forget about it.

KEVIN pulls out a key, he opens the condo door.

                           KEVIN
              I have a better idea.

INTERIOR CONDO. DAY

A sunlit place. Bright colors, comfortable furniture. A place to relax.

ANNE looks around.
                           ANNE
              Wonderful. Is it yours?

                           KEVIN
              Just bought it. Signed the contract yesterday. Like it?

                           ANNE
              Love it.

Looking at everything, taking in the room's calming mood, ANNE walks around.

                           ANNE
              All what it needs are some - touches.

                           KEVIN
              Antiques?

                    ANNE
          Right. There's an outdoor antique market in Santa Barbara,
          do you want me to snoop around a bit.

                    KEVIN
          Yes, I'd appreciate it. After all -

KEVIN takes a deep breath
                    KEVIN
          Will you share this place with me. Will you marry me?

Surprised, almost shocked ANNE faces KEVIN

                    KEVIN
          You're shocked. Forgive me. I know my proposal is a bit
          improper - no, it's highly improper...I know we've known
          each other only for a short time...tongues will wag if you
          marry so soon after you lost Tom. But I love you and I know
          - I hope you love me too.

As ANNE keeps staring at KEVIN, he rushes on.

                    KEVIN
          You're shocked by my proposal. I can tell. Honestly I did not
          dare to ask. But Lil...right, I did not like her at first, but now
          I've changed my mind about her...she's the best friend you
          ever had - and well, Lil suggested that I ask you. So -

                    ANNE
          Shut up...please. Yes...yes...I'll marry you.

Laughing and crying, filled with a new, never before felt happiness, ANNE rushes into KEVIN's
arms
                    ANNE
          I love you.

Passionately they kiss. After a while KEVIN opens a small velvet box. He places the engagement ring on ANNE's finger.

(NOTE: Forward movement Sub-Plot: Anne and Kevin get engaged)

EXTERIOR. OPEN AIR ANTIQUE MARKET. DAY.
There are rows and rows of vendors. Some have their wares spread on the ground. Others
display goods on tables as they sit - like observant toads - under their umbrellas. The lanes
between the displays are narrow and jammed with collectors carrying bags and pushing shopping carts. Mercilessly the sun beats down on dealers and shoppers. The Pepsi-vendor, pushing
his cart, does a brisk business.

ANNE carrying a few shopping bags containing her purch⌐ ⌐ks at a lot of junk. After a while she picks up a plate, considers buying but then puts the plate down and moves on.

She stops at a stall, looks at a Victorian butter dish. Bending down to take a closer look, she bumps into someone.

>   ANNE
>   Sorry.

ANNE looks up.

ANNE's POV . TOM's face zooms in and out, a shrill sound pierces before TOM's face disintegrates into whirling fog. Out of the fog comes a voice -

>   VENDOR (V.O.)
>   Are you all right...let me help you

The vendors face emerges out of the fog. There are other faces, shoppers, and there is - Tom's face.

Back on ANNE. She rubs her hands over eyes and forehead.

>   ANNE
>   I'm fine...thank you.

VENDOR return to her booth. The shoppers disband. TOM walks to the VENDOR'S booth. ANNE keeps watching him.

ANNE'S POV. TOM browsing through some old prints.

>   ANNE
>   Excuse me.

ANNE reaching for a print steps closer. Tom pulls a print from the stack in front of him, looks at it, turns to the vendor.

>   TOM
>   I've got to give you a check...again. How much?

>   VENDOR
>   Twenty five dollars.

ANNE watches TOM reach for his checkbook. He hunts in his breast pocket for a pen. ANNE steps closer.

>   ANNE
>   Tom.

TOM looks up. ANNE touches his hand.

> ANNE
> I recognize you, Tom.

> TOM
> I beg your pardon.

> ANNE
> I know its you. What is going on. I have to know.

TOM hands the check to the vendor, he reaches for his purchase.

> ANNE
> Don't you recognize me. I'm Anne...your...

> TOM
> Sorry Miss, I've never met you.

TOM walks off. ANNE looks after him.

ANNE'S POV. On TOM getting lost among the shoppers.

BACK ON ANNE. ANNE turns to the VENDOR.

> ANNE
> Do you know the man who just bought one of your prints?

> VENDOR
> Honey, I see so many people, I can't remember one face from another.

> ANNE
> He paid with a check.

> VENDOR
> So he did. Why do you ask?

> ANNE
> I think I know him.

> VENDOR
> And..

> ANNE
> I mean, I used to know him...some time ago. There's something I've got to ask him...

                              VENDOR
              Some unfinished business - I guess.

                               ANNE
              And I wonder whether you might be kind enough to let me
              take a quick look at the check he just gave you.

                              VENDOR
              Naw, that might be against the law.

                               ANNE
              I understand. All I want to do is to verify the name and...

                              VENDOR
              We dealers have to be darned careful. One little mistake and
              we loose our permit.

                               ANNE
              Please. It's very important to me.

VENDOR hesitates before she pulls the check from the purse she carries under her apron.
ANNE reaches for the check.

                              VENDOR
              Sorry, I cannot let you see it. The name on the check is Dr.
              Alfred E. White. Does that name ring a bell?

                               ANNE
              No. But my...former friend - might have changed his name. Is
              there any address on the check?

                              VENDOR
              There is. But I cannot tell you.

VENDOR hesitates before she blurts out.

                              VENDOR
              Dr. White is with the University - he told me a few weeks ago
              - he teaches for the philosophy department.

(NOTE: Forward movement Main Plot: Tom is still alive. TWIST)

INTERIOR UNIVERSITY. OFFICE. DAY
A typical faculty office. An elderly secretary sits behind a desk.

                             SECRETARY
              Dr. Alfred E. White - yes, he teaches a philosophy course.
              This is Dr. White, we just hired him.

The secretary points to a row of faculty photos on the wall. ANNE steps closer.

ANNE'S POV. TOM'S photo

INTERIOR PARISH CHURCH. DAY
FATHER O'BRIAN half hidden by votive candles kneels at a side altar.

CUT to ANNE silently praying in a pew.

On FATHER O'BRIAN. He rises, crosses himself and genuflects before he walks over to where ANNE waits for him.

> ANNE
> I know Tom died. I have seen him dead. But yesterday I saw him alive.

> FATHER O'BRIAN
> If Tom is still alive you cannot marry Kevin. You know the Church does not permit divorce.

(NOTE: Forward movement Sub Plot: The Church won't sanction Anne's and Kevin's marriage)

INTERIOR POLICE DEPARTMENT. KEVIN's OFFICE. DAY
KEVIN explodes.

> KEVIN
> ...The man you saw at the antique market...

ANNE gets up, she walks to the window.

> ANNE
> ...was Tom. Maybe his death was faked...

ANNE'S POV. Down on Main Street crawls the late afternoon traffic. Sunlight, feverish, burns on the windows of the office building across the street.

> KEVIN (V.O.)
> Well...maybe..

ANNE walks back to KEVIN'S desk.

> ANNE
> - the body of a homeless was cremated...

> KEVIN
> That still doesn't explain why Tom - if he's still alive - assumed another man's - Dr. White's - identity.

The phone rings. KEVIN picks up.

                    KEVIN
        Detective McGuire...yes, she's right here.

He hands the phone to ANNE

                    KEVIN
        It's Lil.

                    ANNE
        Hi - fine - well sure, I'll be right over.

                    ANNE
        I've got to run over to Lil. Help her out. See you later.

KEVIN and ANNE kiss.

Both walk to the door.

                    ANNE
        We've got to talk. If Tom's still alive -

Another kiss, and ANNE leaves.

INTERIOR LIL'S LIVING ROOM. DAY
Caterers are busy setting up tables, a bartender sets up a bar. Boxes, dishes, people are everywhere. LIL throws her arms around ANNE

                    LIL
        Thanks for helping me out. You're a true friend. I hate to
        leave you with all this   mess -

They walk to the door.

                    LIL
        - but I've got to go to that stupid faculty meeting. You know
        when Dr. Michner, that old windbag whistles...

LIL opens the door

                    LIL
        ... we peons got to run...just keep an eye on the caterers.

EXTERIOR LIL's HOUSE. DAY
ANNE and LIL walk down the flagstone path to LIL's sports car. Lil's high heels click on the
tiles.

                              LIL
              Remember, cocktails at eight and dinner at nine o'clock.

LIL climbs into her car.
                              LIL
              Very European. And don't forget to wear something smash-
              ing.

ANNE's POV, LIL's car speeding off.

ANNE turns and walks back to the house.

ANNE's POV. Seagulls hovering over the magnificent expanse of the purplish-blue ocean. Wings straight and still the birds seem to wait for an event about to happen.

Back on ANNE walking down the flagstone path.

ANNE's POV. A now familiar light orb wavers over the red and yellow flaming flowers border-ing the path. The orb turns to vapor, then a fleeting glimpse of a hand, and now - the ANATHATOS - sign.

Back on ANNE. Puzzled she returns to the house.

INTERIOR LIL'S HOUSE. LIVING ROOM. DAY.
ANNE winding her way around tables and caterers, enters the den.

INTERIOR LIL'S HOUSE. DEN. DAY
ANNE reaches for a paperback, she curls up on the sofa and browses through the book. After a while she puts the book down, gets up, walks to the TV set, turns it on. A football game roars over the screen. ANNE switches channels, now a cooking show is in progress. She clicks the TV set off. She walks back to the bookcase and looks through the tape rack. She pulls out a tape. Puts it back. Then she sees a tape on the coffee table.

CU the tape titled "Musical Treasures"

ANNE puts the tape into the player. The happy sounds of a musical's overture fills the room. Abruptly the music stops. On ANNE during the following, tape recorded conversation. Her face shows fist disbelief, then hurt turning into fear.

                              LIL's voice
              Kevin, we are ready to proceed.

                              KEVIN's voice
              Nothing can hold us back now, darling

                              LIL's voice
              Yes, Anne that dumbbell fell right into our trap. Believed
              you'd marry her. She served her purpose, now let's get rid of
              her.

> KEVIN's voice
> About that - what's it called?

> LIL's voice
> ANATHATOS (and now a giggle) A stands for 1 - N - stands
> for 13 - A stands for 1...Get my drift...

> KEVIN's voice
> And that's connected to -

> LIL
> - that darling little lab of mine. Tell you more later, can't
> wait...to hold you in my arms.

Again the music roars. Back on ANNE. Shaking with fear she hurries out of the den.

(NOTE: Forward movement Main Plot: LIL is revealed as the Antagonist. Significance of ANATHATOS sign. Forward movement Sub Plot: KEVIN works together with LIL)

INTERIOR LIL'S HOUSE. LIVING ROOM. DAY.
Tables have been set up. Boxes and crates have been taken away. The caters have left. ANNE is alone. SOUND OVER: a car approaches and stops.

ANNE at the front door. SOUND OVER: Lil's high heels clicking on the flagstone path. ANNE returns and hurries out of the living room to the kitchen.

INTERIOR LIL'S HOUSE. KITCHEN. DAY
ANNE rushes through the kitchen to the back door. The door is locked. ANNE tries to open a window. The window cannot be opened. She hurries back to the living room.

INTERIOR LIL's HOUSE. LIVING ROOM. DAY
ANNE hurries through the living room to LIL's bedroom. SOUND OVER: keys jingling in the lock.

INTERIOR LIL'S HOUSE. BEDROOM. DAY
ANNE, her breath coming in hard, dry sobs, runs to the window. She throws the drapes aside. The window is secured with iron bars. ANNE knows she is trapped.

SOUND OVER: Slowly, ever so slowly the door opens. ANNE whirls around. She faces LIL.

LIL dances into the room, walks to her bed.

> LIL
> Guess what, Michner canceled the meeting. I'm telling you
> that guy is senile. Why South Coast -

LIL throws he purse on a chair, she kicks off her shoes.

                              LIL
                  - keeps him on, is beyond me.

LIL leaps up on her bed. Yawns, stretches.

                              LIL
                  Thanks for watching the caterers

                             ANNE
                  You're welcome

Slowly, frozen, ANNE walks to the door.

                              LIL
                  Melinda was right, Catherine is old Mrs. Garber's daughter.

                             ANNE
                  Extend youth forever -

ANNE'S voice is tight with fear,

                             ANNE
                  So, after all Sven proved his longevity hypothesis.

ANNE has reached the door.

                              LIL
                  No way. The old dear was not able to form one single
                  scientific concept of his own. All he did was exploit the
                  theory. When Sven became too bothersome I had to eliminate
                  him...kill him.

                             ANNE
                  Tom...he's still alive?

                              LIL
                  You may say so, but now enough of that nonsense. I've got to
                  get some rest.

Lil smiles a devious smile.

                              LIL
                  It's about time you rest, my pet. Stop that foolish nosing
                  around.

LIL reaches under the covers, she pulls out a small gun.

ON ANNE, she stares at the gun.

PULL IN on ANNE

CU Gun, Lil's finger moves close to the trigger.

ON LIL, smiling

PULL in on LIL's hand as LIL pulls the trigger.

ZOOM IN on a tiny flame.

Lil reaches for a cigarette, lights it.

> LIL
> Kevin - our Kevin - gave it to me. Cute, isn't it?

Lil stretches.

> LIL
> See you later.

Frozen, ANNE grabs the door handle, opens the door. SOUND OVER: LIL'S laughter

> LIL(V.O.)
> And don't look for the elusive secret lab. You won't find it.

(NOTE: The above CLIMAX scene (dark moment) leads into the denouement, Act III. Forward movement Main Plot, Anne's life is in danger. Question 9 answered: Lil killed Sven. Forward movement Sub Plot: Kevin deceived ANNE)

ACT III

EXTERIOR WOODED AREA. NIGHT.
The moon breaking through clouds dimly illuminates a rocky hillside.

A car stops, ANNE gets out. She wear black jeans and a black top, Her hair is covered with a black cap. ANNE walks to the back of her car, she opens the trunk. She takes out a camera hangs it around her neck, then she takes out some tools which she secures in the belt strapped around her waist. Next she arms herself with a flashlight.

ANNE gropes her way up the hill. SOUND OVER: the distorted echo of LIL's laughter.

> LIL (V.O.)
> You won't find it - you won't find it - You won't find it -

And now, drifting out, again Lil's laughter.

ANNE stops, she takes a deep breath, pulls the belt tighter around her waist, fights her way through the underbrush.

EXTERIOR "SHELTER". NIGHT,
ANNE reaches the "shelter", she enters through - what once has been - a door.

INTERIOR SHELTER. NIGHT
ANNE flicks on her flashlight. The Flashlight reveals what looks like a kitchen before it focuses on a narrow hole in the wall. ANNE crouches down. She slips through the opening.

INTERIOR TUNNEL. NIGHT
The tunnel is low and narrow. ANNE illuminating the tunnel with her flashlight crawls along.

ANNE'S POV. A wooden door. Her flashlight cuts across it.

ANNE takes the screwdriver from her tool belt.

On the door handle and the screwdriver. Rusty from age and dampness the screws won't budge.

ANNE tries again and again. Sweat runs down her face. She gaps for breath.

Suddenly the walls spin around her. Fighting nausea and fear, ANNE digs her fingernails into her palms. After a while ANNE is able to breath again. She secures the screwdriver back into her belt. Looks at the door.

On the door.

On ANNE reaching for her hammer. She pauses before she attacks the door. SOUND OVER: Hammer strokes - thunder bolts - echo through the tunnel.

On the door. Wood splinters. There is a narrow opening, the opening grows wider. Another thunderbolt of a hammer stroke, and ...the hammer gets stuck.

On ANNE. She pulls.

On the door. The hammer moves a bit.

On ANNE. She pulls harder. SOUND OVER: Metal clattering on the other side of the door.

On ANNE holding the hammer's wooden handle in her hand.

                                    ANNE
                      Why...why...why...

Exhausted ANNE leans against the door.

Again the tunnel begins to spin around ANNE. Steadying herself she holds on to the door handle. Tightens her grip...and...the door opens. Half laughing, half crying ANNE forges ahead.

111

<u>INTERIOR VICTORIAN COTTAGE. BASEMENT. NIGHT.</u>
ANNE's flashlight beams over adobe walls. Narrow wooden stairs lead upstairs. But there is nothing that suggests an entrance to a lab.

ANNE's hands search over the walls. She finds a small recess.

ON recess. ANNE's hand moves a few loose bricks aside. Nothing.

On ANNE. Frustrated she looks around. Walking up to the staircase she angrily kicks some grain sacks aside. And there it is.

ANNE's POV. The door.

ANNE steps closer. She faces a solid steel door. She explores the door. Finally, close to the floor ANNE discovers a dial.

                              ANNE
              ANATHATOS - A stands for one, N stands for thirteen - A
              stand for one ...

CU on ANNE's dialing the safe combination.

The door opens a crack. Heaving, ANNE opens the heavy door just enough to squeeze through.

<u>INTERIOR FREEZER.</u>
ANNE enters. A bright greenish light hits her eyes. Blinded, ANNE steps back, she closes her eyes.

On ANNE opening her eyes.

FLASH CUT: Corpses hanging from hooks.

Back on ANNE staring in disbelief

ANNE's POV. Skin, green plaster - eyes, bulging fish eyes, stare in accusing surprise.

Shaking with fear and cold, ANNE takes out her camera. She snaps a few pictures. Then she steps closer, takes individual pictures of SVEN, SHAWN, CATHERINE and BOB. BOB wears a black robe and heavy black boots.

Tightly holding on to her camera ANNE goes back to the door. Her shoulders pressing against the door, ANNE opens it wide enough to slip though, when a SNAPPING SOUND (SOUND OVER) makes her turn.

ANNE'S POV. Dead eyes boring into her eyes, BOB walks up to her.

Back on ANNE slipping from the freezer.

INTERIOR COTTAGE. BASEMENT. NIGHT
ANNE, fists pushing against the steel, feet pressing against the floor, she fights to close the door, when BOB throws the door open.

ANNE's flashlight clatters to the floor. She tumbles back against the wall, almost looses her balance, but then - gaining momentum - she slams the door shut. SOUND OVER: the latch clicks. ANNE, driven, runs up the staircase

INTERIOR VICTORIAN COTTAGE. HALLWAY. NIGHT.
ANNE runs to the front door. She pulls back the safety bolt located above the doorknob. SOUND OVER: A screeching sound.

ANNE listens. In panic she turns the doorknob. It remains locked. Hands outstretched ANNE rushes through the hallway and enters the living room. SOUND OVER: A creaking sound as the door leading to the basement, opens.

On BOB. He enters the hallway.

INTERIOR COTTAGE. LIVING ROOM. NIGHT
ANNE, on hands and knees scurries to the fireplace. Hides in the fireplace.

BOB enters the room.

The bright beam of a flashlight - ANNE's flashlight - plays through the room.

ANNE'S POV. Unexpectedly the beam of the flashlight hits BOB's ghoulish face. From there the light beam travels to BOB's black boots.

ANNE presses against the wall.

ANNE's POV. Streaks of light first hit a corner of the room then trace over the floor.

ON ANNE. The light beam hits the fireplace, almost reveals her.

ANNE' POV. The light beam followed by BOB's heavy boots, leaving the room.

Back on ANNE, she listens. SOUND OVER: a door slams shut. After a while ANNE leaves the fireplace. She looks around. Walks up to a window, opens it and escapes.

EXTERIOR STREET. NIGHT.
A street inhabited by ghosts. No street light. Not one single lit window on the entire block.

Cautiously, holding herself in the shadows, always expecting BOB to follow her, ANNE walks along.

ANNE'S POV. A faint stream of light seeps through draperies.

<u>EXTERIOR HOUSE, NIGHT.</u>
Shoulders bent, ANNE fights her way through an overgrown front yard and up some steps. Fist clenched she hammers at the door.

> ANNE
> Let me in - - please - - let me in.

The light is turned off.

> ANNE
> Please, there's someone after me.

A window opens a crack. A gun barrel pushes through.

> MAN (V.O.)
> Get going.

ANNE turns and runs. She dashes past another dark house, when she spots an alley.

<u>EXTERIOR ALLEY. NIGHT</u>
ANNE ducks into the alley. Shadowy walls protecting her, she runs to the welcoming sight of a small shopping center. SOUND OVER: Someone whistling the same scale - five notes up, five notes down, over and over. The whistler closes in. ANNE hurries on. She looks over her shoulder.

POV ANNE the alley behind her looms dark and empty. SOUND OVER: A sudden crashing sound.

Back on ANNE her feet pounding the pavement she runs on, suddenly something grabs her shoulder. She whimpers as she forces herself to turn. Hands stiff she touches a tree branch that - hanging over a fence - has caught her sweater.

ANNE stumbles on.

<u>EXTERIOR SMALL SHOPPING MALL PARKING LOT. NIGHT.</u>
Stumbling, ANNE falls against a parked car. She tries to catch her breath, tries to clam down. A shadow falls over her.

ANNE'S POV. Bob, hands raised looms next to her.

Back on ANNE and BOB. Pushing against black cloth, flesh, bones - ANNE bolts back into the alley.

FLASHCUT of a building ANNE has run by but a few minutes ago. A faint stream of light seeps onto the street.

On entrance door.

On ANNE. she grabs the door handle. The door springs open. ANNE slips into the building.

INTERIOR WAREHOUSE. NIGHT.
ANNE slams the door shut. Looks around, tries to adjust to the room's semi darkness.

Feeling safe for a moment. ANNE winds her way around a few crates, when she sees a phone. She dials.

                         ANNE
           Father O'Brian...I...you...

ANNE'S POV. Black boots descending a staircase. ANNE dives behind a crate.

ANNE crouches on the floor. The beam of a flashlight hits her.

                    SECURITY GUARD (V.O.)
           Hey babe, what -

On ANNE and SECURITY GUARD.

                       SECURITY GUARD
           - are you doing here? Get out. Right now.

ANNE throws her arms around the man.

                         ANNE
           Thank you - thank you - thank you

                    SECURITY GUARD
           Are you nuts?

                         ANNE
           I can't tell you how glad I'm to see you.

                    SECURITY GUARD
           You better quit your act, sister. Sweet talking won't help you
           a darn. I know you broke in here -

SOUND OVER: A rock comes crashing through an upstairs window. SECURITY GUARD races up the stairs.

On ANNE. SOUND OVER: sounds of struggle, someone crashes against a wall, there are some muffled screams, furniture topples over. Another heavy thud. A door slams. Boots clatter down the stairs.

                         ANNE
           What happened -

ANNE'S POV. The flashlight playing over black boots descending the stairs - slower...and slower...and slower

                    ANNE
        Everything all right?

ANNE's POV. BOB's ghoulish face hangs over her.

ON ANNE and BOB. For a long time, emotionless, they look at each other. Instinctively ANNE knows what will happen. She is not afraid. She has no emotions left. There is nothing but a void filled with puzzlement: Why me?

                    LIL (V.O.)
        Bob, stop that nonsense right now.

ANNE tries to turn her head. Impossible.

ANNE's POV. Something floats above her, a mouth - eyes - a face comes closer and closer. And now a weightless voice -

                    LIL
        Take it easy - -

Back on ANNE. SLOW MOTION: In shifting, floating movements - almost obscured by ever blinding and then dimming lights a mask slides over ANNE's mouth. Fingers - softly - close her eyes.

(NOTE : Next scene, beginning of denouement I)

INTERIOR LIL'S HOUSE. DEN. DAY
Mist floats across the screen. SOUND OVER: a far away ringing sound. Voices ringing louder and louder.

                    VOICES (V.O.)
        The angels are here...the angels are here...

ON LIL and ANNE. Slowly voices and fog drift out. ANNE lays on a couch. Softly Lil touches ANNE's forehead.
                    LIL
        You gave me quite a scare. You were almost gone. Luckily I
        found you in time.

ANNE tries to focus her eyes. She can hardly speak.

                    ANNE
        What happened?

                    LIL
        Total physical and emotional collapse, my pet. It almost killed
        you.

LIL walks to a tea set and lifts the teapot.

> LIL
> How about a cup of tea?

CU on teapot. The teapot shines like a sacred vessel.

> LIL (V.O.)
> I know why you got in all that dumb trouble -

Back on LIL , she pours a cup of tea, and carries the cup over to ANNE

> LIL
> - last night. You were determined to prove that I committed all kinds of atrocious crimes.

> ANNE
> I found the freezer...and the corpses.

> LIL
> So you did.

> ANNE
> There are experiments on humans.

> LIL
> Wrong. No such experiments are - or were ever conducted. These are not necessary. Immortality is not longer a hypothesis but a proven theory. Immortality does exist.

> ANNE
> It does? In your twisted mind maybe, but -

> LIL
> Let me explain. I'll tell you the truth, I promise.

> ANNE
> Why should I believe you? You have lied to me. You have lied to me all the time. You killed Tom and you've taken Kevin away from me.

> LIL
> Listen to me.

> ANNE
> Words are easy.

                              LIL
          The concept of immortality - not longevity - has been around
          for thousands of years.

PAN to some gleaming Grecian vessels

                            LIL (VO)
          The ritual of immortality is a highly guarded secret. I'll reveal
          it to you: The ritual is a procedure -

Back on LIL
                              LIL
          - that permits an entity to take over a human being by way of
          delating the spirit - call it soul, if you wish - from the body.

                             ANNE
          Like you delate something from a computer's menu. Don't
          take me for stupid.

                              LIL
          Hear me out. During the delating process the human body -

LIL reaches out, she holds up a statue. A soft grey mist floats through the room.

                              LIL
          - turns into a vessel. The entity takes over the vessel. The
          vessel -

On ANNE. Grey mist floats around her

                           LIL (V.O.)
          - never ages. Though after a while it stops to function. Then
          the occupying entity takes over a new vessel.

                             ANNE
          You mean to tell me that by jumping from body to body the
          entity remains immortal? Ridiculous...

Back on LIL. She puts the stature aside and walks back to ANNE as slowly, ever so slowly the
mist diminishes.
                              LIL
          To the average human mind...maybe. The ritual, of course -

Now LIL walks to the bookcase covering an entire wall.

                              LIL
          - is bestowed upon a few carefully selected human specimens
          only.

LIL's hands glide over the books.

> LIL
>
> - men and women who contribute to the world's -

> ANNE (V.O)
>
> Your world - the world of body hopping entities.

> LIL
>
> Don't make fun of the ritual. I'm warning you.

> ANNE (V.O.)
>
> Go on.

LIL walks back to ANNE.

> LIL
>
> I am speaking about men and women who contribute to the
> world's betterment. Top intellectuals.

ON ANNE and LIL

> ANNE
>
> You mean, you're telling me, Bob, Shawn and Catherine
> belong to that choice group of world-do-gooders.

Lil laughs.

> LIL
>
> You've got me there. Those dear ones are what's called
> Lemurs. Emotionless, mindless yet alive creatures who do
> our bidding. Ever so often, to keep their cells from deteriorat-
> ing -

> ANNE
>
> You stuff them into a freezer. I see.

> LIL
>
> Will you please take me seriously?

> ANNE
>
> That's fine with me. So here it goes: Did you kill Tom?

> LIL
>
> No.

> ANNE
>
> You did. Tell me the truth

Red glowing, hissing, laser beams flash through the room

                              LIL
              Tom, the idealist...

Against her will, ANNE nods

                             ANNE
              A runner without perception...

There is a long pause. ANNE keeps staring at LIL.

                              LIL
              Sven was after the ritual for his own glory. Tom...

Again ANNE nods.
                              LIL
              Immortality has to be practiced on a highly selective basis
              only. Tom, unfortunately, wanted everyone to join the
              joyride. Can you picture the consequences?

                             ANNE
              The brave new world.

                              LIL
              That's what he called it when he confessed to Father O'Brian

Again LIL gets up. She walks to her desk. Picks up a photo. From far away the sound of cymbals
comes up.
                              LIL
              Anyway, eager to get to the root of the ritual, he was ready to
              experience the ritual's beginning stages.

                             ANNE
              And you let him to believe -

                              LIL
              - that he were to come out of it alive.

On TOM's photo

                            LIL (V.).
              Right. I destroyed Tom's brain -

Back on LIL. She places the photo back on the desk, as the sound of cymbals grows stronger
and stronger, until it almost drowns out LIL's voice.

                    LIL
        - I released his soul. Now his body serves as a vessel for an
        entity that - presently- goes under the name of Dr. White

Cymbals stop ringing. Everything has returned to normalcy. LIL walks back to ANNE. She
cradles ANNE's hands in hers.

                    LIL
        You are my friend. Help me to bring the dawn of longevity
        and the morning of immortality to the world. I need you to
        continue my work - after I'm gone.

                    ANNE
        Forget about it. You reduce people to specimens. You destroy
        human dignity. I won't help you...ever.

Silently the two women face each other

                    LIL
        That's your final answer...

                    ANNE
        It is.

                    LIL
        Then I have no other choice. I'm sorry. Believe me Anne, I'm
        sorry.

LIL walks to a cabinet. She takes out a syringe and a small bottle. She hold up the bottle to the
light.

ON ANNE She tenses her shoulders.

                    LIL (V.O.)
        First I'll administer an injection -

ANNE Pushes her feet and hands against the couch.   She pushes with all her strength. Inch by
inch, always watching LIL she manages to sit up.

                    LIL (V.O)
        - to destroy your brain, what a waste.

Unable to plant her feet on the ground, ANNE falls back. Motionless she stars at LIL, who
syringe in hand walks up to her. LIL reaches for a cotton ball. Her smile caresses.

                    LIL
        Relax. Don't be afraid, it's almost over.

LIL dips the cotton ball into alcohol, she rubs ANNE's arm. ANNE's eyes widen, a gurgling sound surges through her throat.

> FATHER O'BRIAN (VO)
> Stop that nonsense.

The priest pulls LIL back. The syringe clatters to the ground.

> FATHER O'BRIAN
> We cannot destroy Anne's brain.

(NOTE: End of denouement I, beginning of denouement II. Main Question answered: LIL killed TOM because he wanted to bring immortality to the entire world. Question 4 answered: Tom confessed to Father O'Brian about assisting LIL)

> LIL
> I've tried my best. I've told her about the ritual, but she won't join us. I must destroy her.

> FATHER O'BRIAN
> There's still a way to make her one of us.

> LIL
> True, but I'd prefer not to.

> FATHER O'BRIAN
> Once you took the same road.

> LIL
> That was a long time ago.

> FATHER O'BRIAN
> A very long time ago. Now the vessel has served its purpose.
> It is time the priestess inhabits a new temple. It is time -

SOUND OVER: Brakes screech. Car doors slam

> LIL
> I can't. I won't.

Guns pointed, a SWAT Team charges into the room, KEVIN and the two FBI men follow.

> FATHER O'BRIAN
> You must. There's no other way. Anne is ready. The night she
> found shelter in the vicarage -

> LIL
> The night the birds chased her?

                              FATHER O'BRIAN
                        That night she turned into a vessel.

KEVIN rushes up to ANNE
                                  KEVIN
                          Thank God, you're alive.

ANNE turns away. She resists when KEVIN tries to cradle her in his arms. But KEVIN won't
let go of her. He kisses ANNE's lips, and face and hair. ANNE does not respond.

ANNE'S POV. FBI man I clamps handcuffs on the screaming and fighting LIL.

                                FBI Man II
                        You may remain silent -

                                  LIL
                    What are you arresting me for, you fools?

                                FBI MAN I
                    For the murders of Bob Briggs, Shawn Douglas, Catherine
                    Garber, Sven Johnson and Tom Gerard.

                                  LIL
                        You son-of-a-bitch.

                                  KEVIN
                    Dr. Stanhope, we've found the freezer.

                                  LIL
                        Who -

                                FBI MAN II
                    Father O'Brian gave us a hint.

                                  KEVIN
                    He told us about Tom's explosive confession.

                                FBI MAN I
                    Yes, during his confession Tom Gerard admitted to having
                    participated in criminal experiments.

                                FBI MAN II
                    He even confessed to the location where the "living dead"
                    await their fate.

                                  KEVIN
                    Father O'Brian will you please - -

KEVIN turns around. His POV, the priest has left.

> FBI MAN I
> He was here, when we came in. I don't -

On LIL. An overpowering electric current runs through her body. The FBI man standing next to her is thrown aside. He tumbles against the wall. Rapidly the current spreads through LIL. Her muscles, contacting and releasing, shake like tree branches in a storm.

ON ANNE. Her eyes glued to the spectacle, frightened yet fascinated, ANNE'S bones seem to melt.

Back on LIL. LIL ceases to tremble. SLOW MOTION: A leaf drifting to the ground, LIL collapses. Her hair turns silky white, then - within seconds - to skimpy straw hanging over a shrunken face. There is a toothless mouth, skin as dry and wrinkled as clay. Regardless of the distance between them, LIL's eyes bore into ANNE.

On ANNE returning the look. A silent message seems to pass between the two women. In a gesture of sorrow, ANNE reaches out to LIL.

Back on LIL. LIL'S face disintegrates. Raw bones protrude through decaying flesh.

ON ANNE as excruciating torment shoots through her body. She cringes in pain.

Back on LIL. Lil's body ignites and shoots up in flames, burning and disintegrating until nothing is left but some charred bones.

A moment of stunned silence. Then -

Telephone calls, people shouting, cars driving up - KEVIN holds ANNE even tighter.

> KEVIN
> Calm down, darling, please clam down.

> ANNE
> Let go of me.

> KEVIN
> Let me tell you what happened - please

> ANNE
> I had enough of your lies.

> KEVIN
> Hear me out. Please. You see I'm with the FBI, not with the
> San Louis Police department. About a year ago Washington
> received information about some criminal scientific research
> that, allegedly, involved experiments on humans. The activity
> - Let's go outside -

Establish police officers milling around, as KEVIN and ANNE make their way through the room.

>   KEVIN
>   - as I said the activity was pinpointed to South Coast College
>   and - more precisely - Sven and Lil. I assigned one of my
>   people - Bob. Posing as a new student he infiltrated Sven's
>   group of handpicked volunteers. Shortly after he disappeared.

(NOTE: End of Denouement II, beginning of denouement III. Question 10: How is Father O'Brian involved, what side is he on)

INTERIOR LIL'S HOUSE. HALLWAY
KEVIN and LIL walk through the living room to the front door.

>   KEVIN
>   It was about time I joined the fun. So I went undercover.
>   Became Detective McGuire. Before I left Washington I
>   contacted Dr. Ames, the president of Eastern University. He
>   cooperated fully by offering -

A TV reporter and her cameraman step in front of KEVIN and LIL.

>   REPORTER
>   Detective will you kindly give us -

>   KEVIN
>   Sorry, no comment.

>   REPORTER
>   There are rumors -

>   KEVIN
>   I said - no comment.

>   REPORTER
>   But -

KEVIN opens the front door, he and ANNE exit.

EXTERIOR LIL's HOUSE. NIGHT.
KEVIN and ANNE walk down to the beach.

>   KEVIN
>   Anyway Dr. Ames dangled the carrots of high financial
>   reward and academic celebrity in front of Sven's and Tom's
>   eyes. Then unexpectedly Tom died. I knew he had been
>   murdered. Of course, I suspected Sven, but soon my
>   suspicion turned to Lil. I had to get close to her.

<u>BEACH. NIGHT.</u>
ANNE and KEVIN walk along the water's edge.

> ANNE
> You had an affair with her. In the line of duty. I understand.

> KEVIN
> I'm not proud of that, anyway, I got the information I needed.

> ANNE
> And in the line of duty you did get to know me and you even proposed marriage. I bet there's a wife back in good old Washington -

ANNE'S POV, the ocean. Moonlit waves pound the beach.

> ANNE (V.O.)
> - who doesn't mind your involvement with another woman. After all -

Back on ANNE and KEVIN

> ANNE
> - it's all in the line of duty.

> KEVIN
> I understand your anger.

KEVIN draws ANNE close.

> KEVIN
> I am not married, and that's the truth.

ANNE frees herself, she walks to the water's edge. KEVIN follows her.

> KEVIN
> I love you, and I meant it when I said - I want to marry you.

KEVIN's POV. In front of his eyes ANNE turns invisible

> KEVIN
> Anne...

(NOTE: End of denouement II, beginning of denouement III. Forward movement Main Plot: Kevin is a FBI official, Eastern U. worked together with the FBI. Forward movement Sub-Plot: Kevin did not betray Anne)

BEACH. ROCK AREA. DAWN
Dawn breaks. ANNE walks along. Vignettes of memories, not her own but those of the women who had sheltered the entity now occupying her body, float through her.

FADE OUT on ANNE walking. FADE IN glimpses of LIL's life:

Coming out party at the Waldorf in New York, Horseback rides in Central park, Kissing an attractive man...

FADE out. FADE IN: ANNE walking.

ANNE's POV. The ocean. Dawn breaks, the first rays of the sun touch the ocean.

FADE IN.
Steerage. A woman, screaming, apparently searching for someone makes her way through a group of passengers.

MOVE IN on another woman's face and OVER:

Raised fists, screams, a burning stake. Flames.
(Each segment moves faster)

BACK on ANNE walking. The ocean, azure blue and deep green, glows next to her.

ANNE sits down on a rock.

HIGHWAY. DAY
A limousine drives up. An uniformed diver get out, opens a door.

FATHER O'BRIAN, wearing a suit - not his habit - emerges. He walks down to the beach.

BEACH. ROCK AREA. DAY.
FATHER O'BRIAN walks up to ANNE. LIL's bright smile flashes over ANNE's face.

> ANNE
> I hope you had enough sense to get some decent outfits for me.

> FATHER O'BRIAN
> Of course. Every item was purchased in Beverly Hills.

> ANNE
> Thank you.

ANNE thanks him with another one of LIL's smiles.

ANNE
By the way, how come you told that FBI jerk, Kevin
McGuire, about the freezer and Tom's confession.

FATHER O'BRIAN
To set things rolling. It was time for you, priestess, to inhabit
a new temple, and since - you and I some time ago - had
decided on Anne Gerard -

ANNE gets up, she stretches. Both, she and FATHER O'BRIAN walk back to the limousine.

FATHER O'BRIAN
- to provide a suitable vessel -

ANNE
- and since you are found of dramatics -

FATHER O'BRIAN
I took steps to have Lil Stanhope's body destroyed.

HIGHWAY. DAY.
The driver opens the door. ANNE and FATHER O'BRIAN enter the limousine.

INTERIOR LIMOUSINE. DAY

ANNE
What about our cover assignment?

FATHER O'BRIAN
You are Anna Fiori a dress designer, and I am Armand
Corbin your assistant.

ANNE
So, fashions it is now.

FATHER O'BRIAN
Quite an interesting change from our previous, rather tedious
endeavors.

ANNE
And our destination -

FATHER O'BRIAN
Rome, the eternal city.

ANNE
I love it. Rome here we come.

<u>HIGHWAY. DAY.</u>
On limousine driving along the seashore.

CUT TO: Waves breaking against the shore while end titles roll.

END

PART IV

FINANCING YOUR SUSPENSE FILM

Granted, your Suspense Short slated for film festival exhibition should be financed via "elbow grease", that is to say, everyone involved in the project not only works for free but does contribute a small amount of money. If, however you are ready to produce a Suspense Film slated for theatrical and/or cable distribution you need MONEY, BIG MONEY. You'll approach prospective investors via an OFFERING, while you'll approach a major studio and/or independent production company with a PROSPECTUS. Both OFFERING and PROSPECTUS feature the following basic items. (And now a word of advice: Don't attempt to finance your project without the help of a knowledgeable entertainment attorney. Your brother-in-law who handles divorce cases and litigations won't do. Get in contact with either Los Angeles or New York bar associations as to referrals.)

The following list will give you an idea about your OFFERING/PROSPECTUS must salient elements:

COVER PAGE

Cover Page: Title of your film: ....

Project Description: A Motion Picture Project

Brochure Description: A financing Outline ....

                                Name of Production Company ....

                                Name of Producer ....

PAGE I

List the film's key elements:

- Attached screenplay
- Star (only if a recognizable star has shown interest in your project)
- Topic
- Locations
- Hook (the film's sellable element)

Sales potential: A letter or intent from a reliable distribution company

PAGE II

OFFERING

This statement lists the following entities you are offering your prospective investors:

Limited Partnership. Investors become LIMITED PARTNERS, while the producer remains the GENERAL PARTNER. The LIMITED PARTNERSHIP protects each LIMITED PARTNER from any liability in excess of his/her investment.

Corporation. Investors acquire non-transferable shares of stock in the company.

Investment Contract. The producer/production company contracts with the investors re. interest rates (no profits) to be secured from the invested money.

Joint Venture/General Partnership. A few partners (including the producer/production company) share risk and profits.

PAGE III

STORY SYNOPSIS

PAGE IV
Producer's and director's resumé, if applicable

SCRIPT

BUDGET

1100	Story and Rights		1600	Above-the-line Benefits
	Screenplay			WGA pension (12.5%)
	Idea for Screenplay			Producer's unit
	Xerox			Director's unit
				Cast SAG pension (12.5%)
1200	Producer's Unit			Star SAG pension (12.5%)
	Executive Producer			
	Producer		1700	Production Staff
	Associate Producer			Production Manager
	Legal and Auditing			Script Supervisor
				Production Secretary
1300	Direction			Production Accountant
	Director			
	Assistant Director		1800	Set Design
				Art Director
1400	Cast			Assistant Art Director
	Star			Purchases
	Co-Stars			Rentals
	Supporting			Damages
	3- Day Players			
	1- Day Players		1900	Construction
				Construction
1500	Agent fees			Purchases
	10% Star's Salary			Rentals
	10% Actors Agents			Construction workers fees

2000   <u>Set Operation</u>
        Key Grip
        Grips
        Slate
        Equipment Rental
        Damages and Losses
        Purchases

2100   <u>Special Effects</u>
        Generator Rental
        Oil and Gas
        Fogger
        Liquid Fog

2200   <u>Set Dressing</u>
        Purchases
        Rentals
        Damages

2300   <u>Petty Cash</u>

2400   <u>Wardrobe</u>
        Purchases

2500   <u>Make-up and Hairdressing</u>
        Key Make-up Person
        2 Assistants
        Make-Up Purchases

2600   <u>Lighting</u>
        Gaffer
        Best Boy
        Assistant
        Purchases
        Rental
        Repairs

2700   <u>Production Sound</u>
        Mixer
        Nagra Rental
        Boom Man
        Tape

2800   <u>Camera</u>
        Director of Photography
        Loader
        Camera Package Rental
        Loss and Damages

2900   <u>Transportation</u>
        Grip Truck Rental
        Limousine (Star)
        Trailer

3000   <u>Location Expenses</u>
        Preproduction
        Catered Meals
        Location Rentals
        Fire Safety Officer (if needed
        for Exterior

3100   <u>Editing</u>
        Supervising Editor
        Assistant Editor
        Sound Editor
        Music Editor
        Coding
        Purchases
        Equipment Rentals

3200   <u>Postproduction</u>
        Sound transfer
        Magnetic Film
        Foley
        Sound FX
        Music Recording
        Dolby Stereo Mixing
        Dialog Rcording

3300   <u>Opticals</u>
        Opticals

3400   <u>Music</u>
        Composer, Conductor
        Musicians
        Music Recordings

3500   <u>Film and Laboratory</u>
        35mm Raw Stock
        Developing
        Printing
        Negative Cutting
        Sound Negative Dolby
        Answer Print
        Release Prints
        Coding

3600   Insurance   3700   Publicity
        Cast, Crew   Unit Publicist
        Negative Film   Miscellaneous Expenses
        Third Party Damage
        Camera and Equipment   3800   General Expenses
        Comprehensive and   Telephone
        Umbrella Liability   Office Rental
                                               Office Supplies

*

By now we have walked a long way together. I hope CREATE THE SUSPENSE FILM THAT SELLS has not only answered many of your questions, but has provided guidance and encouragement as well. Creating a film takes lots of hard work. At times you may be tempted to give up. Don't. Don't give up your dream, don't loose patience whether with yourself or your project. No matter what may stand in you way, YOU WILL SUCCEED.

Good luck to you, GOD bless you and your SUSPENSE film.

APPENDIX

ORGANIZATIONS

Academy of Motion Pictures Arts and
  Sciences
8949 Wilshire Boulevard
Beverly Hills, CA 90211

Academy of Television Arts and Sciences
5220 Lankershim Boulevard
North Hollywood, CA 91601

American Federation of Radio and TV
Artists (AFTRA)
6922 Hollywood Boulevard
Hollywood, CA 90028

Directors Guild of America
720 Sunset Boulevard
Los Angeles, CA 90046
110 W. 57th Street
New York, NY 10019

Screen Actors Guild
5757 Wilshire Boulevard
Los Angeles, CA 90036

Writers Guild of America
7000 W. Third Street
Los Angeles, CA 90048
555 West 57th Street
New York, NY 0019

Newspapers
Back Stage
1515 Broadway, 14th Floor
New York, NY 10036-8901

The DGA Magazine
7920 Sunset Boulevard
Los Angeles, CA 90036-3659

Drama Logue
1456 N. Gordon
Hollywood, CA 90028-8409

The Hollywood Reporter
5055 Wilshire Boulevard
Los Angeles, CA 80036-4396

PRODUCTION PERSONNEL

Camera Operators

LATSE LOCAL 644
80 8th Ave
New York, NY 10018

LATSE LOCAL 659
7714 Sunset Blvd
Suite 300
Hollywood, CA 91423

Costume Designers

LATSE LOCAL 892
1349 Ventura Blvd
Suite 309
Sherman Oaks, CA 91423

LATSE LOCAL 705
1527 N. La Brea
Hollywood, CA 90028

Motion Picture Editors

LATSE LOCAL 776
7715 Sunset Blvd
Suite 200
Hollywood, CA 90046

LATSE LOCAL 771
165 W 49th Street
Suite 900
New York, NY 10036

Society of Motion Pictures and TV
Art Directors

LATSE LOCAL 876
11365 Ventura Blvd
Suite 315
Studio City, CA 91604

Society of Operating Cameramen (SOC)
PO Box 2006
Tuluca Lake, CA 91610

NOTES

NOTES